The Granite TOAD

TROY LANE GLOVER

Printed in the United States of America
ISBN: Softcover   978-1-63871-609-9
           eBook   978-1-63871-610-5
Republished by: PageTurner Press and Media LLC
Publication Date: 10/04/2021

To order copies of this book, contact:
PageTurner Press and Media
Phone: 1-888-447-9651
info@pageturner.us
www.pageturner.us

CHARACTER LIST

NOW

DENISE LOUISE GLOVER

Mother of Joseph and James

JOSEPH DANIEL GLOVER

Son of Denise and older brother to James

JAMES MICHAEL GLOVER

Son of Denise and younger brother to Joseph

THERON NEIL GLOVER

Husband of Nelia and father to Maria

NELIA ESMOLADA GLOVER

Wife of Theron and mother to Maria

MARIA ESMOLADA GLOVER

Daughter of Nelia

DOCTOR THOMAS BONZON

Neighbor of Denise and Owner to Sophie the cat

THEN

LOLA ELIZABETH BRANHAM

Wife of Charles and mother to Eugene

TROY EUGENE BRANHAM SR.

Son to Lola and father of Troy and Angela

TROY EUGENE BRANHAM JR.

Son of Eugene and Sara and brother to Angela

RENILDA CAINTIC BRANHAM

Wife of Troy Eugene Branham JR.

WILLIAM BRUCE BRANHAM

Older brother to Lola

SONJA JO CLARKSTON

Mother of Emma

THE GREAT HOUSE SERVANTS

Mamma Gertie ------------Nanny, and Kitchen Chef

Mr. Jonathan ---Stonecutter and brother to Gertie

Miss Mary --Kitchenhand and mother to Josephet

Miss Francine -Kitchenhand and mother to Thelma

Josephet -Kitchenhand and daughter to Mary and Jacob

Mr. Toby --------Senior Barnhand

Mr. Jacob --------Barnhand and father to Josephet

Mr. William -----Butler

Mr. Albert ---Rookery Hand and father to Thelma

Mr. Samuel ------Coach Driver

Thelma -Upstairs Maid and daughter to Francine and Albert

Emma -Downstairs Maid and daughter to Sonja Jo Clarkston

In loving memory of Bernice Lynn Branham

PROLOGUE

March 7th, 1985

THURSDAY AFTERNOON

On the outskirts of a quiet little town somewhere west of Richmond, Virginia, there is a dead-end street called Branham Road. Most any time of day this neighborhood seems empty, with its neatly painted mailboxes and finely trimmed yards. All the houses are brick and in perfect condition. Now, most of the people who live on this street have little desire to do very much, other than, walking their pet and working in the yard.

Most, are retired doctors and other upper, upper middle-income that have just enough money left in their retirement to last them for the next fifteen to twenty years. The houses around here are so close together that even a push-mower would seem like overkill when mowing the lawn. This is why you rarely ever see anyone outside, and that's the way they like it, everyone that is except for the only three children who live here.

Beyond the very end of this road is a good-sized empty lot with a two-story house on each side. To the left is where Joseph and James live with their mother. Maria and her parents live in the house to the right. The two boys are brothers and Maria is their cousin.

Every day these three would ordinarily play in the vacant lot between them, but today the two boys are sitting in their recently trimmed front lawn.

James sat Indian style wearing his super-thin, cotton-poly blend, short-sleeve navy-blue T-shirt with a bright gray image of Albert Einstein on the breast. He rolled up his slightly worn Levi blue jeans like little soup bowls at the bottom of his pants. His off-white hand-me-down Adidas tennis shoes, are loosely laced with black shoe strings.

He is facing his brother with his captivating, bright blue eyes and a discouraged look hanging on his cute little baby face.

Joseph is laying there in his rotunda orange and Jefferson blue track-suit, with his face to the sky. He doesn't seem to mind the wet grass clippings in his hair or on his clothes. He laid there with his arms behind his head and his Adidas, slightly newer looking, tennis shoes, rested on a grass-stained soccer ball. His bright, white shoe-strings are tightly double-tied.

The vacant lot in front of them sits on a hill and tapers down in the back. It gave the children the impression that this space seemed larger than the other yards. This slope also came in especially handy when a stray ball got out of their reach, it would always roll back into the yard and away from the street. At the back of this empty lot is a large, natural, granite stone.

This neighborhood was built about thirty years ago and when the construction crew was leveling out this landscape, they realized the stone was so deep in the ground that they just left it there. Behind the back of this lot is a thin row of trees that separates their neighborhood from the other houses on the next street.

The two boys are sitting in their front-yard watching the Electric Company workers that are in the empty lot next door. If an alien spaceship had suddenly loomed nearby, it would have gone unnoticed compared to what was being placed there right now.

Was it a small playground? -No- Would they like it? -Not now- The lot would never be the same ever again and the children looked to one another for ideas.

A huge yellow truck with flashing yellow lights is lifting a man in a big metal basket, while two other men are installing a transformer on a telephone pole. All of them wearing a highly visible yellow polyester long-sleeve shirt and black cotton canvas pants. All of it in highly reflective silver trim.

This forty-foot, wooden monolith, that the work-men were erecting, defied all the children's logic. Maria a shapely, wavy-haired, pinch of a girl, walked over and somberly sat down on the ground, beside James.

She tied up her long silky brown hair, in a ponytail with a blue and white scrunchy that matched her pastel-blue and white patterned, high-neck cotton sweater and pastel-blue slacks. Her brand new, all white Nike tennis shoes, neatly laced with pastel-blue shoe strings. She looked over at Joseph with her bright brown eyes.

Maria spoke up, stretching her arms in the air, "Why did they have to put it right in the middle of where we play? Why couldn't they just put it on the side of the road like all the other transformers on this street?"

Joseph, a tall drink of water of a boy, shook his head - his lips tight together, "I don't think grownups should run this world." His sparkling, deep-blue eyes always caught Maria off guard.

Maria continued, "They don't think about things before they do them. If kids could run things, we would have at least one lot that stayed empty, just so everybody could have a place to go." The two boys nod their heads with a disappointed grin.

Suddenly a gruff voice rang out, "Okay Carl, Turn it on!" Sparks flew from the transformer and immediately it rang out with a disturbing humming noise.

Then Maria looked at Joseph, "Did you see that? That thing's not safe!"

An older worker-man is standing by the driver-side door of the truck. Smoke from his cigar follows his every gesture as he delegated everyone around him.

Then he yelled out. "Okay guys! It's working fine, let's go!"

As the electrical crew packed up their equipment, the children get up and take a few steps back. The transformer gives out a louder humming.

They all three stood there while the men finish packing, and then James whispered, "Maybe it'll blow up or something!"

As the truck drove away, the new transformer just disturbingly hummed along without failure.

The children could not play in the street, not to mention they couldn't kick the ball anywhere near the house, and did I mention it was the only empty lot in the entire neighborhood that had no trees in it?

The real reason they only played next door was because it gave all of them a feeling of independence, a place where they could pretend, they were out of the eyes of anyone not sharing their imagination and the huge slab of natural stone that stood almost four feet, up out of the ground, was the perfect place to play. This four-foot-wide rock marvel was the center of all the children's games, and it had been everything from a pirate ship to a submarine and even a helicopter.

During the summers, when they could stay out late, its six-foot long surface was a superb platform for putting Maria's telescope on.

Suddenly, the two boy's mother poked her head out of their front door, "Boys, it's time to come in for lunch!"

James looked at Maria, "Wanna come over? We're having 'Hot Pockets' and Cheesy Fries!"

This was an all-time favorite for the two boys. It wasn't a proper lunch, more of an afternoon snack but there was never anything formal about lunch with these two.

"Naa." Maria said, brushing the grass clippings from her slacks, "I think I'll just go lay down for a while, or read a book or something."

Her voice sounded a little listless. Somehow lunch just didn't seem all that much fun compared to the gloom of what -playing outside was going to be like from now on.

Maria swung her arm toward the, not so empty lot, "I guess we're going to have to get used to that, God awful noise over there." They both looked in the direction of the humming transformer.

-Sometime later, back inside the boy's house.

Their mother is in her early forties, plump and round like a well ripened tomato. She's wearing a dark business jacket, that is slightly too small for her, a white silk blouse that is not tucked in the back and black cotton slacks. Her tiny bits of silver sideburns looked like molting feathers on either side of her head.

"Boys!" Denise yelled toward the Livingroom, "Wash up, it's time for lunch!"

While the boys are washing their hands, she placed two, very large plates, on the kitchen table. Slices of homemade fried potatoes hung over the edge, smothered in cheese. A timeless delicacy of the Glover household and the other plate is heaping over with bite sized ham and cheese rolls. The dough has been perfectly deep-fried to a golden brown.

Mrs. Glover spoke as she went back to washing the dishes, "Joseph, I need you to mow the grass in the backyard after you eat and make sure you don't blow any clippings into Mr. Bonzon's yard again, you know how particular he is about his lawn!"

James blurted, over the clanging of dishes and silverware, "Mom! They're destroying our playground with a huge telephone pole!"

James is a very cute little eight-year-old boy, who is very short for his age, which adds to his adorable overall appearance. A very smart young man, his youth and innocence are the only thing holding him back from having the mind of someone much older.

"James!" his mother interrupted, "It was never your playground dear, and it was only a matter of time before somebody moved in next door."

She paused for a moment to wipe a bit of cheese from James's mouth and then continued, "Oh! And I want you to help your brother and make sure there is nothing in the yard that might tear up the mower!"

He nodded his head with a mouth full of fries, "Can I mow?"

Joseph never said a word. He just stood there with the toe of his right shoe on the floor and wagging his foot back and forth like a puppy in front of a food bowl. As he stood beside the table, stuffing two Hot Pockets into his mouth at a time, one fry fell out of his mouth and hit the table.

To anyone who didn't know these two, you might think they are starving, or that their mother never feeds them, but they are hard-playing children and they are always eating. If you left them alone in the house long enough, they might eat you out of house and home.

Beside the front door, there is a small glass dish sitting on a Hepplewhite oak table and in this dish is an assortment of earrings, jewelry and her car keys.

Mrs. Glover grabbed the keys and stood at the front door, "Don't forget, boys, when I get home from work, I expect that yard to look nice for next Thursday!"

She looked out through the screen door, "Does it look, at all, like rain today?" and then interrupted herself, "Oh my God, that car is still sitting in front of your uncles house! Is he ever going to move that thing?"

Joseph mumbled as he walked to the front door, "You need to get over it, Mom."

"No!" She insisted, "A busy yard is a sign of a busy mind."

Joseph looked at her, "Mom, are you reading those old Emma Wilson books again?"

"Watson," She corrected, "And no, everybody knows that, and besides it's an eyesore!"

James complained, "Mom, you're spying on him!"

She shook her head, "Honey, he's a little over a hundred feet from the house, that's not spying, it's just obvious!"

Just then, a brand new nineteen eighty-three black Camaro pulled up in his uncles' driveway. The two watched as the passenger door opened and out stepped Maria, she is adorably dressed in her swing Rockabilly sleeveless black & white polka dot party dress, "Hi, Aunty Denise," Maria said with a wave.

From out of the car stepped the brother-in-law, Theron. He is in his mid-forties, a good head of black and silver hair waves in the afternoon breeze. He is handsomely dressed with his black slacks and silk pin-stripe shirt. It may seem obvious that he has a desk-job by the chubby belly and meaty forearms.

"Hi honey," Denise waved at her niece across the street, "Hello Theron, I see you bought a newer car, so does that mean you're getting rid of that old one?"

"Mom! Rude much?" Joseph nudged, "He told me I could have that, when I'm old enough to drive! You're talking about my future."

"Not yet," Theron yelled back, "I have a friend from church coming over this weekend to look at the transmission!" His deep-blue eyes sparkled as he smiled.

From the front door of the brother-in-law's, house stepped his wife. She is a short, lovely Filipino woman with dark-brown eyes, perfect skin and a shapely frame. Nelia's long black hair hung down to her back. It is obvious by the clothes they are wearing; they must be going out for dinner. Maria clopped up the driveway in her tiny ebony Ester pumps and rushed past her mother and into the house.

"Hello Denise!" Nelia waved.

The short, chubby woman quickly stepped out onto her front porch and walked across the street.

Denise has lived here all of her life. This was her parent's home when she was a child. When her late husband, Troy, passed-away last November, Troy's brother, Theron and his family moved in next door. Nelia has been an essential part of Denise's ability to cope with the loss, and these two have been wonderful friends ever since.

Theron is a retired white, American, Navy man who now works for the government. As a civilian, his security clearance allows him to bid on contract jobs. Unfortunately, that forces him to drag his family to another state about every four years. He joined the military at twenty-one and being stationed in another part of the world, every so often, is the way the Navy raised him.

Nowadays, he feels he has to have a fresh-start every few years, or he feels weighed down and when he stands there in his backyard, all he can think about are all the millions of other backyards he hasn't seen yet.

After seventeen years of service, he has recently been given an honorable discharge. Theron is almost forty years old now, and his career of working behind a desk has increased his recent back problems.

He stood there for a moment stretching while the two women discussed next week's plans. Just then Maria came out of the house, adjusting the slip under her dress.

"Tita Denise, mahal kita!" Maria said.

As the woman kissed her on the cheek, "I love you too Maria." Denise's blue eyes sparkled as she smiled.

Maria is half Filipino and though she was raised in America, she still speaks a fluent Cebuano and Tagalog. After a lot of hugs and goodbyes from everyone, Theron's family is in their car and they pull out of the driveway and whisk away in a black blur and the sound of a racing motor, and shifting gears in the distance.

-Later, in the boy's backyard.

James is throwing every toy in the yard he can find, into a small rusty, metal shed. A Star Wars movie Tonton, a T-47 Air speeder, a Cloud Car also from the Star Wars Empire Strikes Back, An over inflated Wilson Basketball with all the leather peeled off until only the black rubber underneath was left, Several metal cap-guns, A baseball, a softball, a golf ball, A back rim from an old bicycle, a scrambled Rubik's Cube with one of the colors missing, a medium sized plastic Tupperware bowl, an old dirty green cotton two-foot by one-foot-long towel and various other items.

While Joseph checked the oil and filled the push-mower with gas, they are both startled by Dr. Bonzon, who is standing at the fence that separates their yards. A short, kind looking Asian man, he is in his early seventies, and wearing very comfortable earthy colors and brown house shoes, "Here are some fruit and vegetables from my garden. Please give them to your mother."

He hands the boys a medium-sized plastic bag over the four-foot chain-link fence. Then he produces a package of batteries from his shirt pocket, "Joseph, you might need these for the flashlight."

As awkward as that situation was for the two boys, Dr. Bonzon turned and kindly walked back into the botanical garden that took up his entire backyard.

Joseph muttered with a chuckle, "Talk about a busy yard!" and James laughed out loud.

With a hard pull on the thick cotton cord, the mower started right up and Joseph immediately began pushing the rattling mower over the lush dark green lawn.

Aside from Dr. Bonzon's relaxed looking attire of loosely fitted, earth-colored trousers, oversized green t-shirts, and brown house shoes, He is actually a stickler for perfection.

Because of his eager to please attitude, it's very possible that he might be accused of being a control-freak by those who don't really know him.

For example, every night before he goes to bed, he sets the timer on his coffee maker so that it will start percolating at exactly five A.M. -every morning.

Promptly at five 0' clock in the afternoon, he waters his garden which comprises his entire yard, -front and back.

Once a week he irons his bed-sheets and pillow-cases, whether it needs it -or not.

Even though he is a retired psychologist he still makes it a personal indulgence of his to keep up with current practices in the field. With no inhibitions, Tom is one of the leading experts on the expectations of human behavior.

Ask him anything about human psychology and he can explain more than you will ever want to know about why people do what they do. He never stops thinking about what offends other people, including himself. Actually, the only indigenous behavior that has ever escaped the doctors understanding -to date, would be his pet cat Sophie.

In fact, all the well pruned foliage growing outside around his house was planted there by him to entertain his new pet.

However, her hours of recent nocturnal prowling have been leaving pieces of her stiff matted fur all over the house. In order to persuade her into letting him do a lot of needed grooming, he has purchased an endless quantity of catnip. In his never-ending exploration into the mindset of this seemingly cantankerous pet; he powders himself with the herb to encourage her to let him get closer -to no avail.

Every week ends with an exhausting trial-&-error of newly invented pursuits which resulted in, forty-minutes of soothing meditation-music playing throughout the entire house and very large comfortable pillows laced with aromas that, according to the published animal Psychologists, Margo Coffee, in the magazine 'Animals Today', "This should lull any animal, into a physically immobile state of mind." -So far nothing has worked.

The current quandary of Sophie has led him to his latest internet purchase, the talking 'Cat Analyzer'.

According to the television advertisements, it will detect the differences in meow's determining the needs of any animal.

Doctor Coffee's advice has completely convinced Tom that this contraption works perfectly. So, he enforces whatever it tells him about Sophie, despite her seemingly contrary characteristics.

For example, if the cat meows, he presses a button on the Cat Analyzer. The machine states "The animal is hungry!" he puts out a bit more food in her bowl, but for some reason, she won't eat.

The cat meow's again, he presses a button on the Cat Analyzer. The machine states "The animal wants attention!" however, to his surprise, when he tries to pet her, she runs away. The cat meow's again, he presses a button on the Cat Analyzer. This time the machine insists that "The animal is hungry!" He puts out a bit more food in her bowl and she still won't eat. This went on and on until the batteries ran out.

Sophie and Dr. Bonzon are now consulting more professional help. Once a month they go into town to visit a local animal Psychologist where Sophie is learning to better cope with her owner.

CHAPTER 1

The year is 1869, and Emma had a defiant manner springing up inside of her that was sometimes dangerous for a mere servant girl to have. She was seven, and as ole Mamma Gertie had put it, "was 'ripe' for her age." To Emma, that meant she was more mature than most at seven years old. Gertie said Emma's mother had been a brass woman too, so she assumed that she had probably been ripe when she was Emma's age as well.

Mamma Gertie was the old black woman who was nanny to all the children here at the Branham Plantation. Troy Eugene Branham Jr. was one of them. In the early years, Troy's spoiled temper kept those two at it all the time. Nowadays, he was very hard on her, but then again, the Master's son was hard on everybody.

Most of little Emma's responsibilities encompassed the dusting, polishing, cleaning and a long list of other household chores which also included helping out in the kitchen. Of course, she didn't really mind any of the work until it came time to do the Master's Study. No one ever came in here anymore.

Still, anytime Emma was about to go in, she stopped at the doorway and peaked inside, as if waiting for permission to enter. Always, she looked to the painting.

Her eyes slowly traveled from the hearth of the open fireplace to the face above it. Young Emma could not stand to look at the penetrating green eyes of the General's painting. His harsh stare seemed to follow her every move. That is when she had cause to pass through that room, and she was in that room a lot; for her main job was at The Great House.

At the bottom of the pictorial painting, it read "Charles Troy Branham" in all capital letters, as though to emphasize his importance. To her it only increased the fear of that man himself.

The merciless face belonged to the father of her master. "They were evil eyes," she would always whisper, "That face that would never smile." Eyes much like those of her Master Eugene. Of course, to Emma, anyone who had a stern, hard look about them, was considered to be evil.

Stern and hard, two seemingly similar words, yet, defined his character down to every wrinkle behind his intense stare. The man's face had a small, mean little mouth that suited his unsympathetic eyes -perfectly. Whenever she dusted near him, she would always tremble with her usual shiver.

The name of the man was engraved in a precious metal and as the evening sun gleamed through the spotless windows, the shine of the golden plaque beamed onto the floor.

Emma created a game; When the dust in the air floated through the beam, she would always jump over that reflection of light, a game only a seven-year-old might understand.

She had never met this man, Charles; he died in the Navy thirty years ago, long before she was ever born. From what she heard; he was a very *kind* man. One who had a generosity that puzzled her because it didn't seem to fit the face on the wall.

The United States Navy shipped all of his belongings here to his wife. This comprised of three large wooden chests. Lola only opened two of them, and to this very day, she still breaks down into tears when she does.

The third chest, remains locked and still sits at the foot of her bed.

Now his son, Troy Eugene Branham Sr. He had an old chiseled face and matched the one in the picture, but from time to time one could almost catch the upturning of a smile trying to play at the edge of *his* green eyes.

Gertie often said, "Both looked as if their faces might break had they tried it."

On the opposite side of the room is a very tall, standing grandfather clock, with its Roman numeral face. It didn't seem to work, and it never made a sound. Yet it was Emma's daily job to dust every visible part of this clock that was possible for her to reach.

This rather striking hand-painted dial depicted a crouched lion attempting to devour a poor gazelle. The eyes of the lion were not attached and looked like they might move back and forth if it were ticking. The corners of the dial featured two tigers and two horses painted in opposite corners of each other. This weight driven, four pillars, eight-day brass movement and brass hands clock handsomely stood out in the otherwise simple looking room.

Its English Oak case with mahogany veneer trim, rarely needed dusting, but this one-hundred pound, seven-foot-tall machine was twice the size of Emma and always presented a challenge.

Over the fireplace lay a small leather horse-whip on the mantle, its wooden handle -worn from use. There were a lot of things Emma had trouble remembering, but there was plenty she did remember, not the least among them was the whip that threatened her if she dared disobey. She well remembered the first lash of it upon her small body. That whip that lashed out onto her baby skin, leaving a tiny scar on her three-year-old back.

Some said the scar looked like, the number seven; the number of their god Ogun. That it was an omen of being protected by the great gods, if ever there was such a thing. That she had the god's very mark upon her.

She didn't believe it, not for a minute. Never mind the fact that the mark had never been there before the lash of a whip.

In fact, she didn't believe there was a god on the earth or under the earth that cared for her. Nothing in her life had proven that she so much as had any protection at all, let alone anything like a guardian angel.

CHAPTER 2

Right before that indelible day, that unforgettable moment of her beating she remembered Master Eugene as being kindly towards her people, Mamma Gertie had often spoken of his kindness through the years.

The Master's son however, was a different story altogether. His impudent presumptuousness had given him a reputation that most could not define. A very handsome young man; his curly dark-brown hair and beady green eyes could charm most people into just about anything.

When he turned nineteen, he joined the Navy, just like his father before him and his grandfather before him. So, the house servants only had to put up with Troy when he was on shore-leave which usually lasted for thirty days a year.

One morning back in the spring of eighteen sixty he arrived at the plantation, still wearing his Navy uniform and a large white sack thrown over his left shoulder.

All the Yardhands, who were working outside, stopped to greet him, but he just passed them by. He only had one thing on his mind, and that was to see his father. He made his way up to the side entrance. The solidly constructed wooden steps didn't even make a sound when he half-leaped from them onto the porch.

Just to tease the Butler, Troy never entered through the front door. It's not that he had anything against the young man. Mister William was always so very formal in everything he did, and that is the last thing Troy wanted. No more saluting, no more formal anything for one whole month.

Once inside the house everyone welcomed him at the door especially his grandmother Lola, "My, oh my, but you *have* grown!" She said with a warm smile, "Just put your things down here for now and have a seat in the kitchen."

He readily consented to her tugging and followed her to the table.

Lola motioned for a young, black woman to come closer, "Sweetie, please tell everyone in the kitchen to make breakfast. I know Troy has got to be famished after his long journey."

Directly the young black woman lowered her head with a nod, "Yes, ma'am."

"Gramma." Troy said, "That's Thelma!"

Lola shook her head, "At my old age I can never remember all the names of the many hands working here. So, I've decided to just call everyone Sweetie."

"Now! Stand up straight!" She commanded and Troy quickly straightened his posture.

The young Thelma then went into the next room where the Kitchenhands were washing plates and dishes from the night before. This crew of five, seldom rested. They not only had to feed the master and his family but they also had to prepare two enormous meals for all the Fieldhands. Meal-Time, as they called it, was no small feat, and Gertie was the head of it all.

She was a tall, slender woman with her braided hair rolled up tight in the back of her head. She stopped talking and turned around to look at the young woman who just entered the room.

Gertie blasted, "Thelma did you finish wiping the masters table? We got to be ready for Troy and that appetite of his, that boy eats like a Boll Weevil under a Whitney!"

Thelma was still nervously fidgeting with the white cotton cloth in her hand, "Yes, Mrs. Gertie!", The young woman voiced, "And Troy, he's here right now and Miss Lola she say she wants breakfast started straight away!"

Gertie ordered, "Laud sakes child! Why didn't you say so? Fetch Mister Albert in the Rookery and tell him we need all the eggs he's got so far!"

Gertie looked around the room, "And Miss Mary? Go to Mister Jacob and tell him we ain't got nearly enough milk!"

Now, The Hen House was the building where they tended to all the chickens and collected the eggs, they will need each day to feed the many hands working here, but Lola had her own names for things and insisted everyone call it *The Rookery*.

Meanwhile, outside in the bright warm sunlight, Thelma stopped by the dimly lit metalworking shop and squinted inside the doorway, "Master Eugene?" she said, as she entered the noisy building, "Master Eugene?" she spoke louder.

An ear-piercing grinding sound of metal against metal startled her, and she dropped the wet rag she was wrenching in her hands, "Master Eugene, sir!" Thelma voiced above the noise. "Mister Troy, he's here, sir!"

Eugene was standing by the doorway and quickly picked up the moist cloth. After he whipped the straw that clung to it and began wiping the sweat from his brow.

Eugene nodded, "Thank you, Thelma."

Metal shavings were all up and down his arms and his big frizzy white hair was bushed out and dusty from hours of work in the Stonecutters hut. Small pieces of straw hung from his long-sleeve flannel shirt from working in the barn and dried mud clumped up around the edges of his brown leather boots from working in the garden.

As he took a moment to wipe the metal shavings from his arms, he noticed she was smiling at one of the young men and then he handed the dirty cotton cloth back to Thelma.

Several Workhands were pounding their hammers against hot glowing metal cylinders on a steel anvil. One of the younger men smiled back at Thelma, while two other men were rasping their metal files against an unfinished iron rake that was fastened to a sturdy wooden table. Everyone self-absorbed in their work and sweat beading down their gritty necks.

One could always sum-up every sound of the workers into one single word -rhythm.

Every syllable they chose in their dialect, even every step they took is always done with a conscious intentional effort to harmonize with every other sound around them. Everything, all the work, all the sounds, have a rhythm. Djembe' as the workers referred to it was performed in three tones. To them there was no movement without sound and there was no sound without rhythm. This, always brought pleasure to their daily chores.

As Thelma walked out of the building, Eugene turned to the exhausted men, "Alright now, once you finish the last of these rakes, I want you to clean up and get ready for meal-time!"

-Sometime, later.

Eugene and six tired Workhands walked up the red cobblestone walkway, His bushy white hair gently bouncing in the breeze as he walked. He stopped and lifted the lid off of a four-foot-tall wooden water-barrel and plunged his face in; to his shoulders. Five whole seconds went by before he flung his head out of the barrel with a loud, "Howl!" and then made his way up the white painted steps of his house. The rest of the men hurriedly washed their arms and face in the barrel of water.

CHAPTER 3

Troy was still eating a plate full of scrambled eggs and bacon when Eugene walked in. Immediately the kitchenhands turned and grabbed a broom and started sweeping up the dried mud and filth that was falling off of him while two other women helped him into a chair and started taking off his dirty boots.

Eugene voiced around all the fuss they were making over him, "Good to have you, son! After you get settled in, I have something of Grandpappy's that I know you will love to see!"

Of course, the name Pappy was referring to his grandfather Charles, and that is what Troy was always told to call him. He had no genuine memory of his grandfather; his father rarely took him to visit this plantation, until Eugene's father died, but by then Troy was already twelve years old.

Later that evening, after Troy washed up and changed into a more relaxing off-white, all cotton, evening shirt and brown cotton trousers. He made his way through the large impeccable estate, looking for his father. He stepped out onto the luxurious wooden back porch and there was Eugene sitting at a finely made wooden patio table. There on the well shellacked table was a partially assembled musket rifle. -Troy's green eyes lit up.

Eugene sat there wearing similar evening attire except for the long white stockings under his knee-high pants. His long white hair was still wet and combed back over his ears.

"It belonged to your Grandpappy," Eugene said, polishing the barrel with a piece of clean white cotton cloth.

Next to the gun was a one-inch-tall tin cup filled with clear oil. After sticking a bit of his cloth into the oil, he went back to polishing the other parts of the gun.

Troy said with excitement, "Where on earth did you find this?" and sat down beside his father, "The only other firearm on this plantation is your pistol!"

"Oh, that ole thing." Eugene shook his head, "I only used it to run off the coyotes that tried to get into my chickens."

Eugene raised Troy on stories of the Wild West and frankly, a gun was a straightforward way to get you shot but he always taught him the ideology to respect great minds.

"However!" Eugene continued, "Anything finely crafted, has always impressed me. To me this is an ingenious machine, an artform of metal and wood."

Eugene handed Troy the barrel and oily cloth, "Remember that old locked chest at the foot of your grandmother's bed? I finally got it open, and this was right on top!"

Troy looked down the barrel of the gun and examined its outside markings on the lock. Stamped with the engraved image of a crown and two letters V.R.

"V.R.?" Troy questioned. "I wonder what that stands for!"

Eugene explained, sitting back in his oak wooden chair, "Victoria, Regina. Queen Victoria Regina!"

Eugene ran his fingers over his chin and continued, "This is no ordinary rifle; it's a regimentally marked first-Pattern Brunswick. This once belonged to the Elite first Battalion of the British Army. You see there - eighteen thirty-nine."

Troy started assembling some more of the parts together while Eugene went on.

"This is a beautiful example of the First Pattern Brunswick. It's quite an advancement over the smoothbore Brown Bess Musket -this required a newer brand of soldiers known as the Rifle Brigade."

Troy finished putting the handmade thirty-inch-round Damascus barrel into the retained walnut wood by three iron keys along the fore wood. A very solid, darkened shellac finish. Its many small nicks and dings bore witness to its various travels and campaigns with the sixtieth Rifle Brigade.

Troy sat quietly working the strong cocking hammer back and forth. Using his thumb to half-cock and then pulling it down into its full cock position. After taking a long look down the sights, he stood up and aimed it out across the lawn, and then looked the completed rifle over thoroughly.

"Well!" Eugene broke the silence, "I'm very proud of you son, you're becoming quite a man now, a Navy man at that! I want you to have this!"

"Wow!" Troy exclaimed, "Thank you sir! I will take excellent care of this!"

Eugene nodded his head, "I know you will, son, and I've been thinking, I'm getting too old, what this place needs is a younger man to take the reins! I'm handing it all over to you now - this is your plantation!"

The young man stared in amazement, "I don't know what to say, Dad!"

Eugene smiled, "You don't have to say a thing son. It's getting late. I'm going on upstairs and it's getting past my bedtime."

Troy nodded, ran his palm over the wood of the gun and then turned to his father, "You know, I have a few new ideas. It might cost a little more but we could make rifles!"

CHAPTER 4

Cotton was not one of their plantation's many commodities. Troy's father hated the stereotype, associating plantations with cotton. It had been his long-standing belief that Eli Whitney's invention 'The Cotton Gin' would inevitably cause an American Civil War between the states. So, until now, the Branham's staple cash-crop had been tobacco; however, according to Eugene, this was not doing very well lately because of the now growing demand for more cotton and so with their assets now diminishing, Troy got an ear-full from his father about cutting-back on expenses and as his father put it -dead weight.

-Very early the next morning.

Troy was up before the chickens were fed. He was dressed and ready to try out his new rifle. Meanwhile, downstairs in the kitchen, Gertie and the other Kitchenhands were busy preparing for Meal Time.

He marched down the steps with the bottom of his dark brown trousers tucked inside his black leather boots. He stepped into a familiar aroma of burning wood and a sizzling skillet of bacon. With his musket over his right shoulder and sporting a fresh, casual balloon-sleeve cotton shirt. He could hear the commotion going on and walked in.

He smiled at the familiar sight, "Good morning, ladies."

Gertie snapped, "Good heavens, what you doing bringing that ole thing in here for, this ain't the place for it!"

That immediately offended him. Her calling, his new gift, a 'thing' but he held his temper. This woman helped raise him and he had at least an ounce of respect for her, even though he would never let her see it.

Troy stomped over to the cast iron, flat-top Benjamin Thompson cookstove or better known as the Rumford, "I will not fire it in the house, silly woman, relax! What are you cooking there, is that grits?"

She smacked his hand, "Grits, is for the Fieldhands!"

The tall black woman walked around, swinging her hand in the air, "Now! If you want something to eat then you can sit down and put that thing away, what you gonna shoot with that, anyway? There ain't no game round here except them pesky raccoons!"

He smiled with his usual handsome devilish grin, "I might shoot you, old woman, if you don't watch your mouth." A look that had always gotten him out of trouble so many times before.

He turned his head, stomped away and boldly laid his rifle across the kitchen table then he noisily sat down intently with his arms crossed.

Troy spoke over his shoulder, "Then I'll go shoot me a coon if that's all there is around here! Why don't you come with me, Gertie, we'll take one of the hunting dogs with us?"

Gertie turned away and flipped each slice of bacon over one at a time, "We only got one dog and that's Bovine and he's far too old to be running around in those woods a hunting critters for you."

She turned around to him and pointed the seven-inch-long metal fork she was cooking with, "And besides, I'm getting way too old to be playing cowboys and Indians with you!" Gertie had more to say but she had enough sense to stop herself.

Troy got a very long lecture from his dad last night and the last thing he wanted to hear was Gertie reminding him of how she used to wipe his nose when he was just a child.

He jumped up and put his arm around the black woman, "Just exactly how old are you, woman? I'll bet you're probably older than Bovine."

The woman stiffened at the notion. Comparing her worth to a white-haired aging canine.

He pondered looking off for a moment, and then back at her, "Come on, Momma, you're going with me whether you want to -or not, so quit your fussing."

Even after all these years, she still fell for that twinkle in his eyes and those cute round cheeks. She couldn't help but show a little grin.

He looked around the room at the ladies who were standing there and gave Gertie a quick kiss on the cheek, "I am very confident, that these lovely young ladies are perfectly capable of preparing Meal Time this morning, like they have done many, many mornings before?"

CHAPTER 5

With, his musket in one hand and Gertie in the other they made their way out to Bovine's doghouse. There were four other vacant dog houses out here but the dog's brothers and sisters have all died of old age.

They both stood there at the back of his land, far out of the sight of the others. He stood there sporting his grandfather's Brunswick flintlock rifle across his right forearm. The weapon was difficult to load and very time-consuming so he wanted to make sure that his one shot was going to be something worthy of the trouble it was to load.

Troy broke the silence, "Momma, did you know the United Kingdom and assorted colonies and outposts used this musket throughout the world?"

Gertie paid little attention to the gun-facts he was spouting out. She overheard the conversation he and his father had last night, especially the part about getting rid of dead-weight. This was making her very nervous, and the sly comment he made earlier about her being 'older than a useless old hound dog' didn't make her feel any better. She looked around as he continued babbling on about his new gun.

"It's point-seven O four caliber muzzle-loading percussion weighs about ten pounds with an effective range of up to three hundred to four hundred yards!"

She looked at him and then the gun. Her eyes looked deep into his but he never made eye contact.

He just kept going on about that gun, "This musket is still in excellent condition. This two-groove rifling with original muzzle notches placed at the end of the grooves. You know that's for aligning the special ball ammunition when reloading."

What had Navy training done to this young man, has he lost his mind completely? They may have had their differences throughout the years but maintained a certain amount of respect for each other. She refused to show any fear as he stood there rambling on.

Troy continued, "Last night my father handed me the reins to this place, and I got an exhausting lecture about anyone wasting resources and that's when it occurred to me. Anything that has lost its usefulness around here needs to be eliminated!"

Gertie held tight to Bovine's leash as he sniffed at the ground. He was old, but he still had the hunting-spirit in him and eagerly searched for the scent of a raccoon. After a moment he howled into the air and jerked the leash out of Gertie's hands. Bovine caught the faint smell of something and charged out into the forest.

Somehow holding onto that poor old dog's leash made Gertie feel a little secure, but that was quickly jerked from her hands and now she stood alone with Troy. For a moment, the awkward silence made her legs weak.

She found new strength as they strolled together, under the shade of the verdant surroundings.

Occasionally, they could hear Bovine howling in the distance and they casually walked in his direction. The fresh morning air brought her back to life, and she searched her thoughts for something to say. As she opened her mouth, she spoke the only words that hung on her mind.

"Are you going to shoot me?"

Troy stopped walking and looked out over the hillside. He didn't speak a word and just smiled. Being a young military brat, he was very familiar with the term 'Trolling' - which is someone who attempts to lie to you intending to stir up an emotional response, and if you can get someone to believe your trolling lie, that was a bonus to the fun.

In the past, he sometimes had officers giving him a hard way to go. He was often at the butt of many a trolling or nagging stories. Since he was sure that a woman living way out here in the middle of nowhere couldn't possibly know anything about trolling.

He knew he could have a bit of fun with her, and the urge to play at Gertie's nerves was always on his mind, "Gertie!" After a pause, he continued, "Everyone has to earn their keep around here Gertie, so I've decided: which one of you, tree's a coon first, I'll keep, and the other one - well, I'll just have to put-down!"

As he stood there patting his hand against the oval bore, two grooved barrel, Gertie made a mad dash for the woods. High stepping it through the thick brush. Her thoughts racing through her mind; She realized she couldn't outrun the bullet of a gun, and even though Bovine was getting on in his years, she knew she couldn't hunt, not like an ole hound dog could.

Suddenly, a thought came to her mind like a clap of thunder that rolled through her heart.

She whispered to herself, "I'll out smart both of those ole hound dogs, Master Troy and Bovine!"

Then she climbed as high as she could up in the closest possible tree she could find. Time passed by as she sat clinging tightly to the thick branches.

Troy traipsed out through the high brush of the forest for a long time, looking for something, anything to shoot at. He saw a squirrel, but he didn't feel that was a large enough target for a one-time shot and he *could* miss. If only he could spot a deer, that would make a perfect target for a musket of this caliber.

Sometimes, fuzz can build up on the oily gunsight and make it difficult to make a clear shot. So, Troy licked his thumb and raked it over the sight because as everyone knows, "If you can't hit a lick, you just ain't tryin'."

He looked a long time up in the sky, at this point he would have settled for a big crow but there just didn't seem to be anything, at all, to shoot at. Then, that was when he saw her. Sitting way up high in the treetops of a cedar.

At first, he would have to admit, the thought did cross his mind. "A large, distant target that wasn't moving." He chuckled to himself.

His fantasy murmurs quickly interrupted to silence, when he spotted his poor hound painfully limping in exhaustion.

Troy sighed at the sight of the lame old animal and whispered to himself, "All the poor thing had to do, was tree a coon."

Troy then turned his musket, at his favorite old hunting dog and slowly squeezed the trigger.

A cloud of smoke and the smell of sulfur separated sight from sound. Everything seemed to move in slow motion, in a detached moment. The thought that, keeping Gertie on her toes was his favorite pastime. Of course, he wasn't really going to shoot *her*, this poor old, decrepit animal was ready to be laid-down, but Gertie didn't know that.

Troy looked up at Gertie and let out a hearty laugh. He always had a hearty laugh, though it was often at the expense of others. His light-hearted demeanor caused Gertie to let out an uncontrolled chuckle of relief.

Now, he wasn't always like this - he had his moments.

I remember one time, long ago, it was a day very much like every day. Who am I, you might ask? Well, at this point, I can't say. This story was handed down to me, by word of mouth, from generation to generation, and now I'm telling it to you.

Truth be told, the word Bovine was written on the can-goods that Miss Lola always served to the only dog we had. This animal was the hairiest little puppy anyone had ever seen. Nobody ever really knew for sure if the dog was a 'he' or a 'she' but somehow, he ended up with this name.

Now, Bovine was probably the only dog known to humankind that seemed to have the uncanny ability to - smell time.

He had a nose so keen that he knew the intensity of an odor early in the day, and as the day progressed the smell faded. This dog knew, when the aroma had reached a, certain dissipation, it was eventually time for his master to come walking out that backdoor.

Now, young Troy was about twenty-eight years old and he was home on one of his thirty-day shore leaves. He busted out of the backdoor, with a large pitcher of water in hand, but Bovine was nowhere to be found.

Nearby there were two young women beating the dust out of a very large rug. This handsomely made Persian tapestry was twelve-feet-long and four-feet-wide. Its beautiful red, green and blue modern design clearly depicted the taste of the Branham family. Each woman held a three-foot-long, handmade, wicker woven rug-beater. The large flat Celtic pattern was perfect for covering a lot of space at a time.

Troy was wearing his favorite pair of dark, pin-striped trousers and Diamond elastic Y-back Suspenders. His white Chinese cotton, long-sleeve shirt wasn't tucked in all the way and his brand-new light-brown leather shoes shined in the sunlight.

He yelled to the two girls, "Come here! Where is Bovine -it's time for his feeding?"

One young woman spoke up, "Sir, Miss Gertie's been watching him all morning long."

The younger of the two ladies escorted the man out to where the servants lived. Gertie's hut was the very first one.

"She's, *watching* him?" He asked, "Why would Bovine need to be watched?"

The young man's puzzled face turned to Gertie. As they approached the old woman's porch, she was sitting in an old oak rocking-chair and gently singing to herself.

Troy stepped up and gently placed one arm on her porch, "Gertie, what's this all about? Where's Bovine?"

"Master, sir," Gertie whispered as she stopped rocking, "Bovine has hid *herself* up underneath this here porch, and is fixing to have a mess of pups."

Troy whispered as he crept up on the porch, "Her, self?" and sat down next to Gertie.

They all sat quietly as the poor dog whimpered in pain.

Troy questioned like a young child, "Isn't there anything we can do?"

Gertie smiled at the fact that he cared for this animal. She placed her hand on his arm and nodded her head. Then once again she started gently singing and rocking in her chair.

> *"Down where the waving willows 'neath da sunbeams smile, shadow'd o'er the murmuring waders dwelt sweet Annie Lisle; pure as da forest lily, never tho't of guile had its home within da bosom O sweet Annie Lisle."*

To the surprise of everyone there, Troy somberly joined in with his spectacular singing voice, the two harmonized all afternoon, singing songs that Gertie would start.

> *"Wave willow; murmur waters, golden sunbeams, smile! Earthly music cannot waken lovely Annie lisle."*

It wasn't long before Bovine was resting and we heard five tiny puppies, moaning for milk.

A few weeks later, the hairiest of the litter became Troy's new best friend, and he made sure this one was a boy.

Marley, as everyone called him, grew up to be the gentlest and the largest puppy anybody had ever seen; but unlike his brothers and sisters, he never had a temperament for hunting. The loud smoke-filled explosion of Eugene's pistol always scared him and Troy quickly lost interest.

Mister Albert was the only one who realized; the one thing Marley was really good for was locating critters that found their way into the house. The dog was born with his mother's nose and soon learned a valuable trade on the plantation that landed him the sole responsibility of knowing which eggs were good and which ones needed to be thrown out.

Each year as the other puppies grew; Troy would take each one with him when he went hunting. With a three-foot-tall deer-hide leather sack over his shoulder, they could sometimes come back with a raccoon or a squirrel and sometimes they would come back with nothing but a sack full of apples from their orchard.

Troy didn't mind at all. The ability to get away from the fast-paced Navy life was always a relaxing distraction -to just walk around in the woods with no responsibilities.

CHAPTER 6

Meanwhile, in 1985

Present day

In this very small town of Palmyra, Virginia there is a very overcrowded middle school called Fluvanna. This school was so overcrowded that the third through to the fifth grade were all in the same rooms but Joseph, James and Maria loved the fact that they shared all the same classes.

Today is the last day of school just before spring-break. The history teacher is verbally drilling her students, asking the children questions of what is going to be on the next test. She is standing there in her wrap around polyester dress with a cream and black pattern and purple flowers. Her hair looked like an ill formed bristle, almost a short curly mullet of sorts.

Miss Whitefield blasted, "Who was Emma Branham's father?"

A few children raised their hand. Except Joseph, James and Maria who were looking out of the window, at the other children, who were playing at recess. Last night's heavy down-pour, left the puddles of a muddy playground, an easy distraction. Light sprinkles still falling from the occasional wind-blown trees.

The teacher leaned back against her desk. Her stocking feet, firm against the floor. Her shoes were still under her desk. She spoke, commanding the answer to the question.

"Maria!" The teacher announced.

Maria sat there at her desk with her arms inside her manila cotton sweater and wiggling in her seat, wearing a plaid skirt and long tan stockings. By the blank stare it was obvious she guessed at the answer, "Uhm, Charles Eugene?"

Miss Whitefield shook her head, "Miss Glover surely, during one of the unproductive moments of your day, you could have read the whopping twenty pages I assigned for the class to read? You would have known Troy Eugene Branham I was Emma's father."

Now, Maria was getting uncomfortable because the teacher had not taken her eyes off of her yet. She looked for a distraction to soothe her embarrassment - the clock on the wall said 2:30 pm. Why couldn't she just pick on the boy to the left of her, who was tapping a pencil on his desk, but the teacher continued to pick on Maria.

"Miss Glover, how old was Sonja Jo Clarkston when she was first brought onto the Branham plantation?"

Maria said with a confident smile, "Twenty.... something,"

"No, Maria," the teacher scolded, "Can anyone *else* tell me?"

Joseph's attention now returned to the teacher, he did not like anyone picking on his cousin. This was a tactic that the teacher had to revert to, occasionally, to get his attention back on the class.

The young man is eleven years old and has the slightly awkward feel of someone who just recently came into his body and good looks. He is a wry, thoughtful young man who's not quite trusting, his own sudden surge in popularity. He looked very handsome sitting there in his dark-blue sweater and tan corduroy slacks.

The teacher beamed, "Joseph Glover! How old was Sonja Jo Clarkston when she was brought onto the Branham plantation?"

Joseph daunted his answer like it was a question, "Uhm seventeen?"

The teacher turned to the class in frustration, "No, Mr. Glover, though your answer was closer than your cousin's, it was still wrong. Can *anybody* in this class, tell me the answer to number eighteen?"

A lovely curly-haired blonde girl in the front row blurted out, "She was fifteen!" Bunched up around her waist was her pastel pink dress and silk white slip.

Miss Whitefield held her sigh, "Thank you, Lola, but next time, please, wait until you're called on."

Maria stewed in her seat for the rest of the class, muttering the answers to the teacher's questions, trying to memorize them. She hated to be made an example of in class.

The teacher announced, "Now class, I will hand out your report-card grades, even if the bell rings you have to remain in your seats until you get your card. You won't be allowed to leave for recess without it."

The teacher called out, all the children's names, except Joseph and James. So, Maria stayed in her seat. The old gum chewing teacher sat at her desk until all the other students had left the room.

The three grew tense as they sat there, looking at each other, staring questioning holes into the teacher. A long bell ringing in the hallway.

The teacher finally spoke up, "Children!"

She stood and walked out from behind her desk, "If you can't bring your grades up after you come back from spring-break."

She looked down at them from over her black horn-rim glasses, "Then both of you might not pass this grade semester." The two boys nodded their heads in grievance.

The teacher turned to the girl, "Now, Maria I know you're new here, and you didn't have to stay behind, but I know you're concerned about your cousins. Next time, I want you to wait for them outside. Do I make myself clear, children?"

"Yes, Miss Whitefield." They muttered as she gave them their report cards.

Three sour faces slowly walked out of the classroom. Just then, James and Maria saw Joseph smile, and they started running for the monkey-bars outside.

It didn't take long for the kids to forget all about their poor grades - history was never one of their strong suits anyway, and the subjects that fascinated the two boys the most were space and science.

A new game Maria has come up with is taking turns quizzing the other two with random trivia questions. As they sat there on the cold wet swing-sets.

It was Joseph's turn to think of a question, "Okay, how far away is Alpha Centauri from the earth?"

"I know, I know!" James insisted, "Four-point thirty-seven light years from the Earth."

Joseph exclaimed, "Correct!"

Maria questioned, "What exactly is a light year, anyway?"

"It's the same as a regular year." James pointed out, "Just with fewer calories." He added with a chuckle.

Maria smiled, "Did you make that up? Tell me you made that up?"

"No." James confessed, "I saw that in a movie."

Dr. Bonzon sometimes took the two boys fishing but since their Uncle Theron moved in across the street. They have been spending all their time with their cousin Maria. Lately, the boy's moments feel fresher. Maria's energy has given them a life that made everything seem like new.

Maria turned, "Okay James it's your turn." She said with a smile.

James thought for a while as they swung back and forth and then he made a sudden stop. Maria also made an exaggerated stop with her swing to listen to James and his pondering quiz question.

James spoke up, "How far away is Mars from the Earth?" He looked at Joseph with a comfortable grin and then back at her.

"That's a trick question!" Joseph noted, "Because the distance changes from moment to moment."

Maria asked, "How do you mean?"

And then Joseph explained, "The Earth and Mars are going around the sun, like two cars traveling at different speeds on two different racetracks."

"Yeah!" James interrupted, "Sometimes the planets are close together, and other times they're on opposite sides of the sun."

"Ambot nimu." Maria whispered.

"Okay, okay I'm sorry I asked!" Maria insisted, "Joseph, it's your turn.

"What does that mean?" James asked.

"It means, I don't know about you!" Maria explained, and they all three laughed.

Joseph turned, "Okay, James, how far away is the earth from the moon?"

James started swinging, "Oh that's easy ninety-three million miles!"

"Nope," Maria corrected, "its two hundred, thirty-eight thousand, eight hundred and fifty-four miles from the earth." Then she started swinging with a gloating smile.

James looked at Maria, "Do you know everything?"

"Yes, ask me anything!" Maria said with a smirk.

James sat up in his seat and continued, "Okay, how many stars are there in the heavens?"

Maria stopped swinging with a huge grin on her face and glanced at Joseph and then back at James.

"I know exactly how many stars there are in the heavens." She insisted, "There are one hundred billion, four hundred and sixty million, eight hundred and twenty thousand, four hundred and twelve, and if you don't believe me, you can count them yourself!"

All three children let out a laugh as though this were a common joke, they have all heard many times before.

CHAPTER 7

To understand the world of Middle School is to realize that the children feel, there are only three classes of people. The first and most popular are the overly social extraverts. Preparatory or Preppies as everyone called them. Their favorite colors are white, beige and anything pastel. These are the kids who have rich-parents and can afford the most expensive designer clothing. They eat, sleep and breathe sports and have a cheerleader as a girlfriend.

The second are the Hoodlum or Hoods as everyone knows them. These are the kids who are heavily into guns, army fatigues, smoke cigarettes and marijuana. Their favorite colors are black, black and black. They are aware of their style, and they do have a keen sense of social skills but prefer to rebel against any overly stylish or the under socially skilled.

The last class of people called the Knurd or Nerds. These are the kids who don't seem to practice very good personal hygiene. Their favorite colors are brown, mustard, and any shade of green. They think about chess 24/7 and all they talk about are black-holes and anything electronic. They are an unstylish, and socially inept introvert. They would rather sit in their bedrooms reading a book instead of going outside to play.

Joseph and James however don't have rich parents. Even though they do live in a rich neighborhood, their mother works her butt off to put food on the table and her only asset is the fact that the house is already paid off. The boys are very active, they would rather play than watch sports on television but neither one of them are exceptional at anything and as for hanging out with the Hoods, most of those kids have troubled home lives and Joseph and James aren't really interested in smoking or drinking and they actually like their mother.

So, as you can probably tell by now, they aren't very popular in school and they are perfectly happy without all the stress of trying to fit-in somewhere and the only thing they have to worry about -are bullies.

CHAPTER 8

The ride home on the bus

Thomas is a closely guarded secret that most bullies would *kill* to keep, and that is the simple fact that there are *only* four seats on the bus that have a heater-vent. That is to say, if there is a fight to break-out, no one really knows what they are fighting about and that's because these bullies are fighting over one of the four seats and they fought diligently to keep all this information classified.

For, the first time this year Joseph got to sit in one of these seats. He didn't know it, but his height, build, good looks and maturity was intimidating the other students and no one said a word when Maria and the two boys sat down. However, the vent in front of them didn't work.

-Suddenly, a tiny piece of paper came spitting out of the vent and then another.

Joseph looked at James, "Hey did you see that?" and caught the tiny piece in his hand.

Maria looked at Joseph, "It's school paper."

Joseph looked around and noticed Mitchell Pollitt, Jeff Cheatham and Toby Clarke were sitting together and they were the only ones not wearing a jacket.

He pulled out his pocket-knife and used it like a screwdriver and took the screws out of the vent. James reached into the vent-hole and pulled out a hand-sized wad of school paper, then gave it to his brother.

Joseph unwadded it and whispered, "Toby Clarke's homework?"

He reached down inside the vent, pulling out wad after wad of school paper.

-Suddenly *heat* bellowed out of the vent!

"Aww!" Maria whispered with a relaxing sigh, "Warmth! Warmth!"

Toby was about Joseph's age and a bully. Just then, James got an idea and threw a paper-wad toward the front of the bus. Someone picked it up and threw it to the other-side. Some kid smiled, and no one complained, so Joseph threw another and another.

Eventually the two boys had everyone on the bus throwing paper wads -until.

One wad landed up beside the bus driver. She slammed on her brakes, picked it up, turned around and stood up.

The children sat motionless in their seats. Their eyes widened as they waited for her to speak.

"I'm going to open this piece of paper!" She announced. "Whoever is on it, is going to the principal's office."

Toby turned around and gave Joseph a nervous stare. She opened it, stood there pondering with a gaze, wadded it back up, turned and just sat down and drove the bus.

James jerked his head toward Joseph, "Why didn't she do anything?"

Maria whispered, "Nepotism?"

"Is that a Filipino word?" James asked.

Joseph shook his head, "She means, they might be related."

The bus arrived at Branham Road and the two brothers and their cousin stood up.

Toby grunted to Joseph, "You have got to be the dumbest, genius I've ever met!"

Joseph smiled when the boy called him a genius and completely disregarded the rest.

After that day, those three bullies were too busy to pick-on anyone ever again. Now that their secret was out, they fought *everyone* for those four seats ever since. It was peaceful for everyone else, and as it turned out, the best way to keep a bully off your back, is to keep them occupied.

CHAPTER 9

Later, while they are walking home, the wind was dying down and, the air was warm with the afternoon sun. Maria noticed something she didn't hear before, the sound of old rusty steel slowly squeaking in the distance. To the right, far off the side of the road, was a wide gravel path invaded by patches of grassy weeds. Through the six-foot tall leggy-herbage an old, rundown building could be seen.

Maria stopped, "Hey, guys, have you ever been in there?"

"No." Joseph confessed, "I think it's a factory, where they used to make whiskey."

Maria whispered with a sneaky grin, "Wanna go check it out?"

"Yeah!" James blurted, "Can we drink some?"

As they got closer, they could see a large shack on top of four enormous steel columns, rain-water still dripping from its shingled tin roof. There was very little paint covering the old wooden boards that were weather-warn and warped with age.

Maria whispered, "I can't believe you guys have never checked this place out before!"

All around them are several buildings that all have steel pipes coming out the side of them and going into the next building.

Maria whispered as they marveled, "It's possible, large amounts of the whiskey were transported from one building to another using these."

Joseph said, "There's usually an old black guard that sits up there." Pointing to the dust caked shack in the middle of the grounds.

Maria turned with a smirk, "I thought you said you've never been here before?"

Attached to the side of one building was an enormous iron water-wheel. Its twelve-foot-tall paddles slowly turned as the heavy creek water beside it flowed down-stream.

"Apparently!" Maria insisted, "This is where the noise is coming from."

Joseph changed the subject, "Check this out; this must have been their power supply. There must be a generator inside that converted the water into electricity!"

Maria pointed to a small window that was just big enough for someone to climb into, "Look, James! If we hoist you up, do you think you could get in there and open the door from the inside?"

"Easily!" James concurred.

After several fumbling attempts and handfuls of James's muddy shoes, Joseph finally helped him climb inside the building. Once inside, James stood quietly for a moment looking the place over. There were several large places in the ceiling that were falling through. The gaping roof provided ample lighting as James made his way over large pieces of fallen rafters and metal shingles.

Maria whispered through one of the fist-sized holes in the otherwise thick wooden wall, "Do you see a way to open the door?"

James whispered through the hole, "There's a bunch of stuff piled up in front of it, like somebody was trying to block it up from the inside!"

Joseph and Maria look at each other and then back at the big rusty metal door.

"That means there must be another way in!" Joseph said, "Look around, is there a way out of the room?"

A gigantic twenty-foot-long generator took up most of the room, slowly squeaking as its axle turned. There were several long, heavy-duty electrical cables leading from it through the wall and as James climbed around the rubble, he spotted the dark shape of an open doorway.

As his eyes adjusted to the dark in the dusty room, he saw tall stacks of wooden boxes reaching to the ceiling. At the top of one stack there was another opened window. Somebody placed the crates perfectly. To James, they looked like enormous steps, where he climbed to the top. Now out on the roof he looked around the edge of the building where he saw Maria and Joseph whispering to one another.

"Guys!" He said, in a raspy whisper, "Up here!"

The other two used some steel pipes that were leaning up besides the building. They used this to help them climb on top of the roof, where James showed them the window that he climbed out of.

"Oy, baho!" Maria whispered to herself.

"What does that mean?" James asked.

"Stinky." Maria explained.

The room stank of old smells that neither of them could recognize and the dust filled their lungs with every breath. They could hardly see where they were going.

Maria whispered, "It's a warehouse."

Joseph walked up to a crate that seemed to have fallen apart over time, "Let's see what they're warehousing." And reached in and pulled out a tall bottle covered in straw and dust.

Joseph whispered, squinting at the label on the bottle, "It's too dark in here; I can't see what it says."

James held it up, "Peach, Schnapps, liquor, but I think they spelled liquor wrong." He whispered looking at the bottle.

Maria corrected, "That's liqueur."

She looked at Joseph, and he raised his eyebrows twice, indicating 'let's keep it!' They both looked at James, and Joseph sat the bottle down on the cool dry dirt floor.

Maria whispered, "What else did you find in here, James?" rubbing her hands together.

James pointed, "There's another room over here guys, there's a gymongrous generator in here."

Joseph slipped the bottle of schnapps into his backpack. Maria stood between the two boys to make sure James didn't notice.

Maria grunted, "Wow! That thing has got to be as big as our living room. Wouldn't it be cool to have this as our clubhouse? We could have electricity and lights and everything!"

CHAPTER 10

All of a sudden, the sound of two trucks pulled up outside, and James started shaking as his eyes got wider.

Maria motioned with her lips, "What are we going to do?"

The loud rumbling from the trucks outside deafened the moment. Joseph looked around and noticed another doorway. The large metal door wasn't open wide enough for him to squeeze through and paused for a moment. With his teeth tight together and a huge squinting grin he waited for the timing of the squeaking water-wheel and shoved on the door once then waited for the right moment and then shoved again. Each time, it gave out a moderate squeak until it was wide enough for the kids to make it into the other room.

Just then the engines were silent and they could hear two men talking by the door. James held his breath, as they could see the men through the holes in the wall.

The men walked around talking about seeing some kids playing nearby.

The children made their way in the opposite direction they saw the men walking and made their way across the cluttered room. Maria could see several boards in the wall had fallen out into the tall grass outside and pointed to it.

It was easy for the three to crouch out into the afternoon sun and once outside they started crawling through the tall wet weeds. They could hear the talking men getting further and further away. Finally, they found themselves back out on the road and walking like nothing had ever happened.

Maria spoke as she let out a giggling sigh of relief, "Oh my God, that was close!" and caught up with Joseph.

When they made it, back to their house, they saw their neighbor Dr. Bonzon standing out by his mailbox.

Maria waved with a smile, "Kumusta Mr. Bonzon, how are you doing?"

The old man nodded, "I am very well, but I'm worried about Sophie. She has not been eating her food." He said as he took a small package out of his mailbox.

"I promise I haven't been feeding her!" James said, "Maybe she's been eating mice or something!"

The children smile and wave as they took off running all the way to the end of the street. Maria didn't stop there, and they followed her past the freshly dug mud of the new electrical pole all the way to the back of the vacant lot.

Joseph collapsed against the large stone slab and James climbed all the way on top, The rush of the whiskey warehouse escapade was still fresh in his veins and somehow being on top made him feel safer than just standing beside it.

Maria sighed with relief, "Have you noticed how his cat smells different lately?"

Joseph looked at her, "Like a foul smell?" he said jokingly.

"No!" Maria chuckled, "Just, different. Maybe like, mint?"

James interrupted with an exhausted breath, "We just went on an awesome adventure with nothing to show for it."

"Well not exactly, nothing!" Joseph enlightened and raised up and sat down next to James. From his backpack he pulled out an old dusty dark-brown bottle with a colorful label.

Joseph read aloud, "French liqueur's Peach Schnapps, seventeen-proof, bottled nineteen fifty-four. This thing is about thirty years old!" He said, as he handed it to Maria.

Maria blew dust from the bottle, "We'll save this for a special occasion!" She insisted and handed it to James.

"Is it whiskey?" James questioned, peering into the bottle.

Maria shrugged her shoulders, "Seventeen-proof, I doubt it, but I've never heard of peach Schnapps. Maybe it's like a type of wine-cooler or something."

The two boys looked at her with surprise at her knowledge of drinking.

Maria nodded, "Both my parents are palahubog, I know a lot about different kinds of alcohol."

"What does that mean? "James asked.

"It means both my parents drink." She explained.

Maria raised up, "I'll see you guys later on tonight. Okay? Right here?" The girl expressed, placing her hand on the granite surface.

The day was getting hotter in the afternoon sun, and James took off his jacket. Just then a nineteen eighty-five sky-blue Audi 5000s came pulling up in the boy's driveway. With a familiar honking on the car horn, the boys came running. This was something their mother always did when she wanted them to come and help bring in the groceries.

As they were bringing the groceries out, Sophie jumped up on the hood of their car.

Denise alarmed, "Shoo! Shoo! Get your claws off my car you hairy thing!"

"Mom." James informed, "She smells the food."

Joseph included, "And she feels the warm hood of the car."

Denise shook her head, "I don't like that animal, it hates me!"

"Well." Joseph spoke, "You did hit her with a broom once."

James agreed, "And one time you tried to pitch hot water on her."

"I don't care!" Denise confessed, "Get that thing out of my yard!"

James picked up Sophie into his arms and walked toward his mother.

A resounding, "No!" Denise jumped back, "Get that filthy thing away from me."

Joseph looked at the cat in his brother's arms, "Well, she is looking a bit nappy lately."

James raised his nose, "And she does smell funny." And put her down on the ground, "Sorry, Sophie."

Their mother quickly walked into her house.

"Why does mom hate Sophie?" James asked.

"Hate?" Joseph scoffed, "I think she has a fear of cats!"

James chuckled, "Maybe mom was a dog in a previous life."

The two laughed out loud as they each carried a large brown paper grocery bag into their house.

Sophie used to live with the Glover family but after Denise's husband passed away, those two females didn't want to have anything to do with each other ever since. Now, the very kind Dr. Bonzon took little Sophie in, but every year about this time, Sophie just seems to act a little wilder than usual.

CHAPTER 11

FRIDAY AFTERNOON

Denise grounded Joseph and James to the house. Not just because of their low grades in history-class, but also because of the grass-stains on their new school clothes. Meanwhile, she went across the street to visit Nelia for a while.

In the living room, the walls had Allwood two-ply veneer panels. Depicting the images of long wooden planks with black-lines between each panel. In the corner sat a burnt-orange Larson leather recliner with push-button release. On top of the television are a clutter of family photos in eight by ten wooden frames. On the wall, over the couch are two paintings. One is of a boy wearing all blue and the other is of a girl wearing all pink. Both are works by the painter Thomas Gainsborough.

Joseph plopped down on the Roche burnt-orange leather Sofa-couch wearing a white all cotton T-shirt and blue-jeans.

"James, see what's on channel three." Joseph demanded.

James stood in front of a brown and beige seventeen-inch wide by twelve-inch high, Sharp Television-set. He stood there turning one knob with a 'click, click, click'.

The commercial announced, "It certainly is a big bun! It's a big fluffy bun. Where's the beef?"

"Let's see what's on channel forty-one." Joseph demanded.

James turned the knob on the television with a 'click, click, click, click."

The television show announced, "Gilligan, very briefly, the Kupakia words to free a prisoner are, Pulu see bagumba! Now hit the words hard and sound like your mad."

"Okay, James. Leave it here." Joseph insisted.

James laid down on the deep forest-green wall-to-wall carpet, with his hands behind his head. He is wearing Levi blue-jeans and an all-cotton sky-blue T-shirt with the image of several super heroes on the breast.

Over their heads hung a stunning all glass and chrome, thirty-four inch wide by thirty-two inch high, twelve bulbs, chandelier with incandescent lights in the shape of a candelabra.

"Pulu, see, bagumba!" James whispered to himself.

The television show announced, "Gilligan concentrate, your vowels are in serious trouble!"

Joseph jumped up, "Are you hungry James? I'm gonna make a sandwich."

"Yea!" James exclaimed, "She didn't say we couldn't eat!"

-Later in the living room.

They each came back with a plate-lunch. A sandwich, a slice of apple, two cookies and carrying a tall glass of milk.

The television commercial announced, "Trying fun new craft-ideas around your home!"

The show depicted a young girl hollowing out an eggshell by blowing through a tiny hole made in it, while the girls' mother poured melted-crayons into the egg.

The commercial announced, "You too, can make your very own egg-shaped candles."

Joseph looked at James, "Let's try that!"

"Yea!" James agreed, "We have all kinds of old broken crayons in the toybox!"

The two forgot all about their prepared lunch. Scouring the bottom of the toy box for any color crayons they can find.

-Later in the kitchen.

James is painstakingly poking a tiny hole into an egg with a needle while Joseph is warming up several, different colored crayons in a metal cooking pan.

"Check this out James." Joseph insisted, "if you mix every color together, you get brown!"

James amazed, "Cool!" Then went back to gently blowing all the contents of the egg into the sink.

James excited, "Hey, we can make Mom, egg-candles for Mother's Day!"

"Make that hole, on top, bigger." Joseph insisted.

James held out the egg with both hands, as Joseph slowly and carefully poured the hot crayon wax into the little eggshell.

"Wow!" James noticed, "It's getting hot." And propped it up in the sink with a towel.

"What is that sound?" Joseph asked.

The two boys look at each other and then back down at the small egg in the sink.

A low rumbling came from the egg. Suddenly there was a loud -BANG!

The egg exploded crayon-wax all over the kitchen in a perfectly symmetrical pattern of dots. James just stood there, shocked for a moment. Both of them covered in brown dots.

"Holy crap!" Joseph yelled.

"Joseph!" James exclaimed, "Look at your shirt! It's a perfect pattern of dots!"

"Look at your face!" Joseph insisted.

The two boys spent the next hour scrubbing every single dot they could find -until!

Denise came walking through the front door, "Boys I'm home! What have you been into? Are you making lunch for yourselves?"

Their eyes widened as she came walking into the kitchen. She didn't notice their chicken-pox faces as she washed her hands in the sink. The two started back toward the living-room.

"Boys?" Denise questioned.

"Yea, mom?" James asked.

Their mother puzzled, "Where did these polka dot curtains come from?"

Joseph calmly turned around by the kitchen doorway, "What curtains?"

"I didn't, buy, polka dot curtains." Their mother insisted.

James turned around behind Joseph, "They've always been polka dot Mom!" and left the room.

"Yea, Mom!" Joseph insisted, "They've always been polka dot. You've, just never noticed."

A resounding, "Mom!" James yelled from the living room, "Are we still grounded to the house?"

Joseph stood in the kitchen doorway, "Yea, mom." Joseph asked, "Can we go outside?"

Denise yelled, "Yes! You're still grounded! But not to the house."

A resounding, "YEAH!". Came from both boys as they grabbed their jackets.

Denise insisted, "Stay around the house young men! I mean it!"

"We will!" Joseph yelled as they made their way out the front door.

CHAPTER 12

Meanwhile, at Doctor Bonzon's house.

Maria has an interesting new summer job – cleaning Doctor Bonzon's house. He told her he would be out of town until late and asked if she would watch his house. Maria showed up in her pastel green Kwik Sew all cotton jogging suit and green tennis shoes, At the front door she squatted down and looked in the flowerpot. There was the key to the door just where he said it would be.

A large, one and a half foot, woven reef hung on the front door with a small bird's nest at the bottom. As she stepped up on the porch, she realized a bird built it because there were two small blue eggs inside.

Also on the door was a note which read, "Please use side door"

-At the side entrance.

Even though it was in March, Dr. Bonzon's Christmas lights were still strung up around the doorway and down the black cast iron rail that went all the way down the length of the red brick steps. The air around the house smelled like different flowers and fresh mulch.

When she slowly stepped through the big wooden doorway, she could hear an unusual sound coming from inside the living-room. It sounded like two distinctly different animals.

"Rat rawl rat raw rut."

Short cat tones emanated from the other room followed by quick sharp chirps that were all cut short, like they might come from an injured bird.

"Chir, peet, chir, pit, up."

As Maria quietly tiptoed through the living room, she realized the back-door was left open. This, of course, seemed very odd considering the fact she knew Mr. Bonzon was not home.

"rawl rut raw rawlt."

As she drew nearer to the door, she could see Doctor Bonzon's cat sitting at the edge of the porch with her back to the door. "Was there something wrong with the animal?" She wondered to herself. "Was it sick?" Maria could also hear another animal on the porch and she stepped to the right to see what it was.

"Pit Chir, up, peet, chir, pit, up."

To Maria's surprise, there was a small blue-jay, and the two appeared to be talking to each other. She was shocked because Maria's understanding of cats and birds was that one tries to kill and eat the other.

Maria spoke up, "Sophie?" and the bird quickly flew away.

As Maria came to the screen of the back door, Sophie turned around and stretched her back and claws.

The cat resounded, "Meow!" and walked to the screen.

Maria knelt down in the floor and stared at the cat through the mesh screen-door. The cat immediately began licking its fur.

Maria opened the door and the cat just stood there. The girl slowly began closing the screen-door until Sophie felt it was the right size opening and slipped into the house.

Most of the day went by uneventfully and Maria ended up falling asleep on the Lorenzo studded Greyish Brown high-back chair, until a voice awakened her in the room.

"Out, out." She heard.

The cat gracefully leaped onto the back of the chair. When Maria opened her eyes, Sophie was on her shoulder.

Maria blinked in disbelief, "Did I just hear you say, 'out'?"

Sophie climbed down into her lap, "Meow." The cat insisted.

Maria thought she must have been dreaming and got up, as she walked to the back door, Sophie walked with her and quickly shuffled outside as soon as the door was open. The young girl stood there for a minute quietly watching Sophie sit at the end of the back-porch facing the lush surroundings. Maria could feel the warmth of the sun on her face and stepped outside to see what the yard looked like. Most had only seen it from the street and this job opportunity was a perfect excuse to quench her curiosity.

Driven in the ground were several, six-foot-tall, wooden stakes, in the middle of three-foot square, wooden frames. These, one-foot-tall, wooden frames boxed in, lush, growing tomato plants that were growing up the stakes. Large, fully grown tomatoes hung from the vines that were tied to the stakes by cotton twine.

Six, eight-foot-tall, wooden fences had green, long-beans growing up and hanging from the tops of the fences. The beans were growing so lush and so close together it looked like six very tall green hallways.

Several, three-feet around, wooden flower pots sat in various places in the yard. Maria counted eleven of these three-foot-tall pots. Each of them had eight-foot-tall, palm-trees growing out of them.

On the ground, strawberries were growing in four more, three-foot square, boxed in frames. This overcrowded little yard was a botanical maze of small pathways made of neatly placed brick walkways.

All different kinds of flowers were growing throughout the entire backyard in different sized flower pots. As Maria stood there gazing at the many wonderful colors, she could understand why Sophie enjoyed just sitting here on the back-porch.

Around every tree several beautiful flowers were planted and boxed in with a one-foot-tall wooden frame.

The cat stretched its back and claws and then turned to walk in front of the door. Maria stood up with her arms over her head and stretched her back. As soon as they both went inside, Sophie ran and found a place to hide for a nap.

Once Maria walked into the kitchen, she saw a refrigerator that was covered with small notes and greeting cards. In the center was an eight and a half by eleven-inch, sheet of paper. It was being held there by a magnet that looked like a plastic notepad.

"House Instructions." Maria read aloud.

"Water all the plants outside.

Do not water anything in the house, I will do that.

If you see fallen plant-leaves on the floor, do not throw them away.

If there is anything rotting in the refrigerator please do not throw away.

There is a plastic box by the kitchen sink.

Only feed Sophie once and only when she's hungry.

Get the mail from the mailbox.

There is a duster in the pantry, dust the furniture and the hanging pictures.

Please straighten any that might be crooked.

There is chicken in the refrigerator and food for you to eat in the pantry.

If you feed Sophie human food, she will not want her own food."

While Maria walked around the house with the duster in hand, she didn't really notice any dust. The living room was all in antique dark wood that looked like they had imported it from a foreign country. Two, plush, couches sat on opposite sides of the room with a flowered pattern and they looked like they never sat on them, except by Sophie. Little cat hairs covered all the furniture.

Twelve small flower pots of orchids decorated the room and on all five coffee tables. Next to the inside wall was a baby grand piano that looked like the same wood as the furniture. On top were many small picture frames of his family and three children. All of them very well dressed, and every couple had one baby.

Down the hallway Maria could hear a voice in the kitchen. She ambled down the hall past the front door.

"Now, now."

As she turned the corner into the kitchen, she saw the cat sitting next to its food bowl on the floor.

Maria spoke confidently, "I'm not asleep this time." She was certain, she heard the cat speak.

The girl squatted, "Now, I know I heard you say 'now'"

The cat rubbed up against Maria's leg, "Meow" the cat said.

"Can you say please?" Maria asked.

She sat down on the floor beside the animal and began running her hand over the cats back, "Oh, you poor baby - your hair is getting so matted."

On the floor was a plastic container marked 'cat food' it looked like it was written with a black Magic Marker. As the cat purred, Maria opened the container and emptied a bit of the cat-food into the animal's bowl.

The girl questioned, "Come on, can you say please?"

The cat just quietly nibbled at its food for a moment and then shook its right paw and walked away.

Suddenly the doorbell rang, and Maria could hear James and Joseph outside, talking. When she opened the door, the two were grinning from ear to ear. Straw was hanging off their dark cotton jackets, and she noticed speckles of dried mud at the bottom of their blue-jeans. She also saw muddy footprints trailing up behind them on the brick steps and the concrete porch.

"Come on, Maria!" Joseph said, "Let's go for a walk!"

James interrupted, "Yeah, and can we come in? I'm thirsty."

She held out her hand, "No! You can't come in here, there's mud on your shoes!"

She then looked at Joseph, "I'm sorry guys I'm house-sitting. Mr. Bonzon is paying me fifty dollars to watch his cat for the day."

Joseph exclaimed, "Oh man! That is so bad!" To a child, the word 'bad' is a good thing showing he was envious of her job opportunity.

Maria encouraged, "Come back later when you get cleaned up."

The two boys turned, "Oh man!" James complained and the two walked down the steps and out into the quiet empty street.

-Later

Maria ran her finger across a shelf of books, the way a child might rake a wooden stick across a picket fence.

She whispered to herself, "Crossroads by Brenda Griffin." Said the name on the cover, "I think this might be an interesting read."

She plopped down on the living room couch, reading the book. Again, she heard that same high-pitched voice coming from the other room.

"Out, out."

Maria sat for a moment in amazement as the cat rubbed up against the backdoor. She concluded that somehow this animal has been trained and got up off the couch to let Sophie outside.

It was getting late, and the boys never came back. The hazy sunset grew dim, and the warm night air made her remember summer was on its way. The house was getting warmer and so she opened the two windows in the living room and went back to reading.

Later that evening Maria awoke to the sound of someone calling from outside.

"Troy, Troy." The distant voice in the dark repeated.

She straightened up on the couch and listened intently out of the window. "No one should be in Mr. Bonzon's fenced-in backyard. Perhaps it was a friend of his, and they didn't know he was away." She jumped up and bounced for the backdoor, but there was no one there. She stared out into the dark yard for a moment listening to the wind gently blowing through the trees.

Maria went back to the couch and listened again to see if she could hear someone. She turned out the light, so she could see the yard from the street lights. After a moment, there was a distinct motion in the window.

"Troy, Troy." The high-pitched voice sounded.

Maria recognized that same sound from the cat and quietly crept up to the window. There, sitting in the window was Sophie looking anxiously at the young girl.

She opened the window, and the cat leaped in and immediately went to her food, nibbled a couple of bites and shook her right paw at the bowl and skulked off, to find a secret place to take a nap.

-Late that night.

The front door opened and Dr. Bonzon came walking through, awkwardly pulling a large luggage-case on wheels. He threw a small stack of mail onto the living room coffee-table and continued pulling the luggage case.

He said calmly, "You forgot the mail."

Maria rushed to him, "Oh I'm sorry, I forgot that on the list. Can I help you with that case?"

"Yes," He said calmly, "Please take it to the top of the stairs." His voice sounded exhausted, and he spoke with an Asian accent.

CHAPTER 13

FRIDAY NIGHT

The two boys got grounded again for coming home with mud on their shoes and pantlegs. They were sent upstairs, without supper. In their room they were sulking on their beds. James laid there in his all cotton long-sleeve black and blue Batman Pajamas with matching pants. Both of their thick comforters depicting a collage of Star Wars images. The room was dimly lit by their matching R2D2 nightlights. Joseph laid on his bed in his all-cotton white T-shirt and Navy blue and red plaid flannel sweatpants with the word 'Virginia' down the right leg. He sighed as he stared up at his X-Wing Fighter model hanging from the ceiling by pieces of black thread.

They didn't talk about the pulsating hum coming from the lighted pole next door, even though it annoyed them both.

Suddenly, a light beamed in across their window. James rose; there it was again, a beam from a flashlight.

"Joseph!" James whispered hard, "Is it Maria?" Both of the boys sprang from their beds. and Joseph snatched a flashlight from his nightstand drawer.

After a series of flashes, "G, N, D." Joseph decoded Maria's flashlight message.

With James's intense stare, "What does that mean, Joe?"

Joseph sank down to the floor under the window, "It means she's grounded too."

James with a more puzzled look, "Why is she grounded, she don't have bad grades?"

Another series of beams lit up their bedroom. The boys signaled back, "W, A, T?". They waited for her message again.

Joseph complained, "O, U, T? Is she crazy? We'll get caught if we sneak out now!" He sat the flashlight face down on the floor between them.

"I don't care." James whispered, "I'm going." He had an intrepid air about him as he handed Joseph the flashlight.

"L, O, T." Maria whispered to herself and then turned to get her sweater. The clock on the stand read, "12:49."

The three met outside in the vacant lot. The dark handsomely disguises James as he ran out across the empty lot in a tattered Batman cape.

The two boys stood there barefoot in matching blue jeans. James still had on his Batman pajama-top and Joseph is wearing his white T-shirts.

Maria was wearing her longs-sleeve, cotton, pastel turquoise pajamas and white wool sweater. "Hey, guys." She whispered, and presented the two boys a small square Tupperware dish, full of spring rolls.

"Thanks, Maria!" James said, with a large piece in his mouth.

"What is this stuff?" James asked holding a spring roll in his hand.

"It's called Lumpia." Maria looked at James.

"Shhh!" Joseph warned, "Quiet, come on."

The children ran to the back of the lot, far out of the reach of the utility poles light. Maria's shoes flip-flopping as she ran.

They walked to their favorite climbing rock, which had been there for as long as they could remember.

James pulled up his Levi blue jeans. Maria raises her eyebrows at him nonchalantly standing there with his worn-out old cape flapping in the night air. Joseph just shrugged his shoulders as she looked to him for answers.

Maria shook her head, "Ambot nimu."

Maria spoke in the dark, "Guys, my dad said this lot won't be vacant for much longer. A young couple is going to build a house here soon."

"Oh no," James cried, "They can't! Where will we play?"

"Shhh!!" Said the other two, "Quietly James," Joseph grunts just above a whisper, "I can't believe this, first school, then we get grounded and now this!"

Joseph looked at the other two who are chewing, "Let's all agree, no matter who moves in here, we are going to *hate* them. Even if they have a kid our age, he's our *mortal enemy!*"

Maria nodded her head, "That's right; they're taking the only place we have to play, away from us."

James agreed with a nod, "Besides, even if they have kids, they won't have a place to play either."

"That's right!" Joseph concurred, "And *we* will not play with them either! -Right?"

James nodded his head, "Hey, look at that! A falling star." He pointed.

The other two turn in time to see several more, shooting across the night sky. Then the wind gently pulled the clouds across the bright moon.

"Oh yeah!" Maria said as she pushes her hair back behind her left ear. "I almost forgot there's going to be a meteor shower tonight!"

As they sat there staring up at the night sky Maria, spoke up, "Guys, how can stars just fall like that?"

"Stars don't really fall." Joseph enlightened, "Stars are really millions and billions of suns, which are so far away that they look like tiny white dots."

James agreed, "Yea, falling-stars are really space rocks from what's left-over from other crumbled planets."

Maria grinned, "Oh really?" She said with a smile.

He stood there with his hands on his hips like a superhero, "Really, really! Would a man in a cape lie?"

They all start laughing and head back across the lot.

James leaned over, "Maria, I'm glad you moved here."

Joseph put his arms around the two, "Hey, guys, let's meet here tomorrow, we can still play frozen catchers?"

Maria put her arm around Joseph, "Hey yeah!" She added, "We can use the telephone pole as base!"

CHAPTER 14

SATURDAY MORNING

Very early, before the television station ever started, James was sitting there in the floor. He sat there in front of the TV, staring at the Station Identification color-test Sign, waiting for what he has always waited for every single Saturday morning since he can remember. He is waiting for the cartoons to start.

Joseph and James would always argue over which channel to watch, so their mother came up with an arrangement the two boys could agree with. "Whoever gets up first, gets to choose the channels for that Saturday."

Ambling down the stairs Joseph made his way to the refrigerator. He stood there, holding the door open. He stared into the open refrigerator for a minute and then shut the door. Silently made his way into the living-room and plopped down on the couch.

He spoke up, "I had a really weird dream last night, this big horse was trying to eat grass through a fence but it was too far out of his reach. I wonder what that means?"

James nodded, "You're hungry."

Suddenly the television started its broadcast station, "TV eight, WCHS Charleston, People you can count on!"

After several commercials, Joseph and James were closely enthralled in every cartoon that came on. Looney Tunes Bugs Bunny and friends, Wile E. Coyote and The Road Runner.

They didn't move when their mother finally got up around ten o'clock in the morning. Challenge of the Gobots, Super-friends, The legendary Super Powers. Transformers, Heathcliff, Battle of the Planets.

It wasn't until she yelled from the kitchen, telling the two boys, "Breakfast is on the table! I have to work today, bye boys, stay near the house!". The two boys jumped up and ran for the front door. James gave his mom a big hug around her waist.

"I love you mom!" James exclaimed.

Joseph hugged her as well and she kissed the two on the cheek, "I love you too mom, bye-bye."

Their mother went out the door with a piece of toast in one hand, a coffee thermos in the other and her car keys in her mouth, "I love you too boys, be good and do the dishes that are in the sink!"

One went to the bathroom and the other went to the kitchen. Moments later the two are at the kitchen table, Joseph is eating his favorite scrambled eggs with sausage. James is sitting with a medium-sized plastic purple bowl. With a large yellow box of cereal in front of that.

To a child, the back of a cereal box was his morning newspaper, even though he has read it every morning since he opened the top. That is unless there was a toy in the bottom. In which case, the box would be upside down so he could get the prize out first.

Joseph ate a bite of sausage, staring at the front of the cereal box, "So, how do you find Captain Crunch?"

James spoke with a mouth full of Crunch Berries, "You find clues with the detective kit."

James stared at the red letters on the back of the box, "Hey Joe, why is 6, afraid of 7?"

Joseph shrugged his shoulders, "Why?"

"Because 7 ate 9!" James explained.

Joseph unimpressed, "So, why do you have to share a $1,000,000 reward?"

James smiled, "Hey Joe, where can an elephant sit in your backyard?"

Joseph quickly, "Anywhere he wants too!"

"Okay." James insisted, "What is black and white, black and white, black and white?"

"What?" Joseph asked.

"A penguin rolling down a hill!" James laughed.

"Okay." Joseph spoke, "Why do cows wear bells?"

James grinned, "I don't know."

"Because their horns don't make noise!" Joseph laughed.

Joseph exclaimed, "Knock, knock."

James's grinning, "Who's there?"

"Cows say!" Joseph announced.

"Cows say who?" James asked.

Joseph laughed, "No silly! Cows say MOOO!"

James laughed so hard; milk came out of his nose.

CHAPTER 15

SATURDAY AFTERNOON

The day is beautiful and warm, the birds are chirping and a dog is barking in the distance; however, the three are not having a very good day at all. Early that morning, a truck unloaded, wrapped stacks of bricks and bound piles of lumber, to be used for the new house that is going to be built here.

Joseph stood there in his Adidas tennis shoes and still wearing the same clothes he slept in the night before, "How can we play frozen-catchers with all of this *stuff* in the way?" Joseph complained, "let's move all of these bricks to the edge of the lot, so we can play."

Maria wore her pleated, green and white circle skirt and an old pair of Nike tennis shoes. She shook her head, "That would take days, and this isn't our playground anymore Joe, my dad says it belongs to the *Watson's* now!"

James is still wearing his Bat-Man pajama top, a pair of Levi blue jeans and Adidas tennis shoes. He is wandering toward the back of the lot, looking through the freshly overturned dirt.

"James!" Maria yelled out, "Come back over here!"

Maria often mothered James like he was more of a son than a cousin. He looked down just in time to see a rock that looked very similar to a frog. When he bent down to pick it up, it leaped from him.

James staggered when it moved, "It's just covered in brick-dust or something."

The frog leaped again but not before James can snatch it up. It amazed him when he opened his hand only to find he's holding a black rock, "It looks like a frog; it looks just like a frog!"

On the other side of the lot, he can hear Joseph is still rambling on about how he hated all the changes to their favorite place to play.

Maria turned around to look for him, "James, you're wandering too far; come back over here!"

While his brother and cousin still complained in the distance, James stood there for a moment with stone in hand, looking for the little frog that got away. He turned and whispered to himself.

"I wish we could all have a place to play where no one would bother us."

A brilliant flash of green light startles Joseph and Maria to a sudden silence, when they both realize James is gone. The two ran where they last saw him standing.

Suddenly, another brilliant flash of emerald light, and there they see James, walking from a distance, petting something in his hand.

Maria looked at Joseph, "What just happened?"

The young boy exclaimed, "Come on guys; I found a really cool tree for us to play in, it has a real treehouse and everything!"

He is excited and walked back toward the end of the lot. Joseph and Maria look at the thin row of trees that separates them from the other neighborhood.

Joseph caught up with James, "Which tree?"

"Come on!" James explained, "I'll show you, there's an old rope ladder, and a really awesome creek with craw-dads in it and everything!"

Maria finally caught up with the two boys, "Which tree are you talking about?"

Suddenly, there is a brilliant flash of light.

James spoke up, "It sounds like TV static!" He yelled.

"The air!" Maria said, "It tastes like sandpaper!"

Joseph frowned, "It feels, like thunder!"

Suddenly, it was silent. Then, the three children were standing at the bottom of a hill with only one tree in front of them.

"That tree, right there!" James pointed.

The ambiance of a gentle stream of creek water immediately caught their attention and the wind blowing through the leaves on the big old Oak tree.

It looked so inviting, the three hopped on large stones, which seemed to be placed there just for this purpose. They crossed the creek and stood under its magnificent view. A morning fog that still lingered beneath the tree added to its majestic appearance.

The two boys ran over to the tree. Maria turned to look back at the empty lot and then back at the boys.

She shook her head, "That treehouse looks so old guys; I don't think it's safe to climb up there."

She wandered around the old tattered structure while the two boys' uninhibited discovery made her feel uncomfortable.

James yelled out, "Joseph, check this out!"

He showed him how the old rope that lowered a drawbridge still worked perfectly. The wide walkway leading up into the old treehouse was dusty, a few bad boards, but soundly put together.

Joseph excited, "Come on Maria, there's a table and chairs, and a swinging bed!"

Maria watched them set all the wooden chairs back around the little table, "That's...that's very interesting," she managed.

"Is all of this a wonderful dream?" She thought, "Or will it suddenly turn into a nightmare?"

The place had a feeling of a total surreal about it. She could hear the wind blowing through the tree's over-head. The water in the creek behind her, tinkled gently downstream. The air smelled fresh like a morning in spring, but still something seemed so unreal about this place.

This riveted Joseph, being a young man who was good with his hands, began testing the stability of every board. As he made his way through the different apartments of the treehouse, he noticed that whoever tied all these ropes used special knots.

"Bowline", he whispered to himself, "Wow! That's a good double-half-hitch." He said as he tugged on the rope.

James was completely at home and satisfied as he plunged into play. The swinging net-bed was a perfect spot to take it all in.

Maria was still reluctant as she made her way to the lowered drawbridge. There on each side of the entrance she noticed two broken flower-pots that still had some dirt in it.

A subtle detail that might have gone inconspicuously unnoticed by two overly excited young boys. She found this inquisitive enigma was shedding an intriguing idea.

"Ano ba yan?" She whispered to herself.

The notion that a girl might have played here, once upon a time, almost disarmed her as her imagination envisioned a marvelous castle in the trees. Goose-bumps went up both her arms.

Suddenly, she snapped out of it and spoke up, "I don't know about this, guys, does anybody know exactly how we got here? I mean, this place is so old and run down and how did it get here, it's never been here before?"

James came lowering himself down in front of Maria on a rope. "I know how we got here!" James pulled out a small rock from his pocket.

Maria's eyes widened at the intricate carvings on the small stone in the boy's hand.

"It's a magic rock, see?" James smiled. "We can come here anytime we want!"

Maria shook her head at the rock and then marveled when she noticed the stone moved.

Joseph interrupted their conversation by swinging in for a landing, "We can fix this place up and make it our own hideout!"

James looked at Joseph with skepticism, "How can we fix this place up, we don't have any money?"

"We can take some of the lumber from the lot!" Joseph explained, "They won't miss it - they've got thousands of boards, and besides, they owe us. They are taking away our only place to play!"

Maria took the hard stone from James's hand, "Joseph have you seen this thing?"

James looked at Maria with a pleading grin, "Please Maria, please, please, please, please?" She looked at the begging child and smiled.

"Okay! Maybe they won't miss just a *few* boards and maybe some nails! But right now, we need to get back! We don't want anybody to come looking for us, they might find our hiding place."

At first, the two boys didn't want to agree, "Go back? Now? We just got here."

"Come on James." Joseph concurred, "She's right someone might find our new hideout."

James sighed, "Okay, but can we come back tomorrow -right?" James asked as he rubbed the little stone in his hand.

Suddenly, they are walking from the back, of the now, dimly lit lot. Moths are now fluttering around the lit utility pole, and the transformer is buzzing as usual.

She looked at the two boys, "Have we really been gone so long?"

Maria's Father opened the door at her house, "Maria! It's time to come in for supper! Come on, honey, get washed up!"

Maria looked at the two boys -puzzled, "Guys, we were, only gone for a few minutes -Right?"

Joseph agreed, "Twenty- or twenty-five-minutes -tops!"

James looked at the other two, "So... what does this mean, what time is it now?"

Maria shook her head, "I don't know but I'm guessing we've been gone for maybe six or seven hours!"

CHAPTER 16

Meanwhile back in

July 9th 1860

The two Branham's, father and son, went to the Town Square for the first time this year. This was to be the last ship to bring Africans into the New World. The ship landed in Mobile Bay Alabama and it brought cargoes of the remaining, farther north that same year, to Richmond, Virginia, near their plantation.

Troy Branham Jr. was thirty-three years old now, a young man in his prime. He stood there in his long-tailed burgundy walking coat, black trousers and high black leather boots. He was silently watching while a young black couple was being brought out from a rustic building and displayed upon a large wooden platform.

When fourteen-year-old Sonja and her seventeen-year-old brother were brought out, Troy paid little attention to her. He was looking for strong bodies to do the work as Fieldhands.

The auctioneer cried, "Who will purchase these two? This male, about seventeen years old weighs approximately two-hundred forty-five pounds, and stands six-foot three inches. Surely, he has the strength to lift, five-hundred pounds without breaking a sweat. Agile, strong, and loyalty are his trademarks; and a definite asset to any owner."

The audience chuckled in amusement at this last phrase; as the auctioneer knew they would, and then he turned to the young black girl. Sonja stood there with a humiliated posture; her eyes never left the ground.

The auctioneer finished, "The female; possibly, fourteen-years-old, weighs one hundred fifteen pounds, and stands five-foot-five inches!"

It was certain the male would be the cause of this sale. However; it was the auctioneer's job to get the most amount of money possible for these two.

He announced, "Who will begin the bid for these two? Do I hear fifteen hundred notes?"

Troy could barely contain himself as the auctioneer final finished his sales-pitch, "To heck with the girl; the boy himself was worth at least a thousand notes." He whispered to himself.

Troy bellowed out, "Eight-hundred for the boy!"

This boy could do the work of two or three men, and young enough to give him service for many years! He would have to bid high for this one, he was sure.

Old man Branham cut in on his thoughts, "Son, that young man there might bring you some good money. I'd be willing to bet my entire plantation, that in a cock-fight, he could stand up to any man in the county. You could be a big winner with a Rooster like that."

A man spoke up, "I'll give you two hundred notes for the girl and an extra eight-fifty for the boy!" One bidder bellowed. It was Clarence Whitefield. His plantation butted up against the Branham plantation, and the Branham men knew what Clarence did with his females.

Eugene leaned to Troy, "You know Whitefield's always bragging about that big one he's got on his place. His fighter is the only thing that keeps Whitefield from going under. That man has won him every fight Whitefield's put him in and won him a lot of money."

Young Branham bellowed, "I bid nine hundred notes for the boy!"

Troy frowned. He didn't care for Whitefield; nor did he care what the man did with his women; it was only a dog fight to him, Whitefield had caused personal problems for the Branham family, problems that had cost a significant sum, and he wanted that boy!

Eugene voiced, "Don't let that old geezer outbid you son; the boy is still worth the price of them both."

Out of the corner of Troy's eye, he noticed Whitefield's smirky grin. This was nothing more than a game to him, the smirk that hinted, he would probably lose.

Whitefield yelled, "Nine-fifty for the lad."

Whitefield didn't really want that boy. His interest was the girl, but he couldn't help himself from rivaling against the Branham's. No one else was bidding; no one dared.

The feud between the Branham's and Whitefield's had been ongoing for twenty-three years now, and the community knew better than to try to get between them. The feud began with the elder Whitefield and Branham, and was simply passed down from generation to generation.

Old Joseph Hacky started, "Three hundred! For the girl." His voice carried more than he realized.

Whitefield's fighter killed his best man in a fight, and the bet was for two adolescent females. The fight was fair enough, but he hadn't liked Whitefield ever since. Joseph always believed Whitefield was an arrogant winner. It didn't really bother him to lose the girls but the arrogance of Whitefield was just too much.

No one wanted to get on the Branham's bad-side; no one at all, except the idiot who was openly bidding against them. Many men licked their lips in excited anticipation over the 'boy', but all were afraid to speak up.

CHAPTER 17

It was rumored that old man Whitefield could make a lot of trouble for a body, and the man who was an enemy of the House of Branham was frowned upon by all. Hacky silently rooted for the Branham's to beat Whitefield out of this one.

Young Branham thundered, "Two thousand notes! for the boy."

The auctioneer cried out to the crowd, "Two thousand, two thousand; do I hear twenty-five hundred notes?"

Whitefield mocked, "Twenty-nine hundred; two thousand five-hundred for the boy and four-hundred for the girl!"

He hoped Troy would give up. He knew, The Branham's had no possibilities for matching him on a monetary level. Whitefield looked quickly over at the two who were speaking in hushed whispers. Then Clarence grinned at Joseph as though Branham was going to let those two pass.

Branham indeed, had finished. The day was hot, and he wanted to get back home. There was a man meeting him this evening about a horse he wanted to purchase, and he grew tired of standing in his own sweat.

"I ought to just let them go; let Whitefield have them." Troy thought to himself.

He could draw a certain amount of satisfaction from the bizarre amount of money he forced the old man to spend. Two thousand-nine hundred dollars on just two servants. He chuckled to himself at the thought.

The excited auctioneer blasted, "Twenty-nine hundred, twenty-nine hundred, can I have three thousand, do I hear three thousand?"

Whitefield boasted loudly to a man on his right, "That girl's going to fit in right nice on my place." He guffawed loudly at his own joke.

The auctioneer looked hopefully towards the Branham's who looked to be leaving. He yelled slowly, distinctively, into the air, wishing for another bid, "Twenty-nine hundred bank notes; going once; going twice?"

Once again Whitefield yelled over the noise of the crowd, "See you at the cock-fights Branham!"

Troy overheard the boast. Whitefield had always grated on his nerves; in fact, even before the deal, he cheated him out of. He would love to put that man in his place. He stamped his walking stick in the dusty ground.

Troy turned facing the auctioneer, "Four-thousand notes -for them both!"

You could have heard a pin drop. No one moved; even the wind seemed to be stunned into immobility. Even his father stared, stupefied. Had his son gone mad?

What manner of insanity would cause anyone to spend four-thousand banknotes for two servants? The crowd turned to him slowly. Not a man among them, lost their gaze on Troy. Did the man have more money than even they thought?

It was unthinkable; a person could buy five or six for that price.

As for Young Troy Branham, he even surprised himself. A man completely in control at all times and he squandered this kind of money on a couple of servants? Well, he had already made a public announcement of his foolishness, but he would let no one even suspect that he didn't know exactly what he was doing.

He caught his father's look of surprise, but he knew he wouldn't say anything in front of all these people. To be sure, his actions would be remarked upon on the way home. But it was young Troy's plantation now; his father had handed him the reins. The elder Branham's health was slowly receding, and Eugene was glad to have a strong capable heir to take it over.

His son walked up to the auctioneer and signed his signature on a four-thousand bank note, cursing himself with each stroke of the quill that bound him to the agreement. The crowd murmured amongst themselves; there must be something about the 'boy', or perhaps the girl, that Mister Branham knew, and they did not.

Old Joseph Hacky knew why and stood there gloating with his arms crossed at Whitefield's look of disappointment.

Now, let it be known, for the days to come, young Branham made his favoritism toward Sonja plain for everyone to see.

CHAPTER 18

One day while reading the *Winchester Evening Star* newspaper, the father and son were in the Den discussing President Buchanan and his claims of equality for all. While young Sonja came into the room and brought two plates and gracefully placed them in front of the two men.

"I like this guy Buchanan." Young Troy voiced.

Eugene looked at his son, "Don't put any faith in Democrat's, son."

Troy stood up, "This could be the end of slavery dad."

Gertie walked in with two wooden bowls of soup and placed them on the plates. Then the two women walked back into the kitchen.

Eugene shook his head, "His efforts to find a compromise in the conflict between the North and the South will fail to avert a Civil War!"

Troy sat back down at the table, "No, I want to make a statement with this mans' plans."

Eugene frowned, "What do you have in mind, just letting them all go to town? Most people today won't be able to accept this kind of change, son. These people are safer here than sending them out into that hateful world."

Sonja returned with a small wooden box and placed it on the table. From out of box, she placed a glass pitcher of water and two glass cups.

Troy thought for a moment, "A small statement. Isn't that where it really starts -small?"

Eugene leaned back in his chair, "You want to just free one of them, as a political statement?"

Troy corrected, "Not just political but a statement to other plantation owners that the Branham family is in favor of the President's plan of equality."

Gertie walked in with silverware and a small wooden plank of bread.

Eugene shook his head, "And you already have someone in mind?"

Troy glanced at Sonja, "A free woman, living here, of her own free-will. That would send a good message to the other plantation owners."

Eugene sincerely looked at the two women, "Isn't that right Gertie, you *are* all family to us! All right then!" He smiled, "let's put the paperwork into motion!"

Sonja's brother was not so fortunate. His presence here at the plantation was to fight for money. Even though he was a big strong man, he did not have the will to kill another person. Sometimes there was so much riding on these tournaments that they got way out-of-hand. No one's life is expendable, not for any reason and Troy secretly saw this as a small way to pay Sonja back for the loss of her brother Joseph.

-Later in Eugene's Study.

Eugene sat at his large wooden desk with quill in hand with a parchment in front of him, "Young lady, do you understand what we're planning to do here?"

Troy sat next to the desk on a plush cushioned Ottoman. Clarkston as it read on the side, "I love this seat! I remember this was how I learned to walk, from pulling myself up on this and it's still as wonderful as ever."

Sonja sat in a hard wooden chair opposite Eugene, "Does this mean I am free to leave?" The father and son glanced to one another and back at the young woman.

Troy cleared his throat, "Now, Sonja, you don't want to leave us, you're like family to us now."

Eugene leaned in, "Miss Sonja, do you have a full-name in mind that you would like?"

The young woman stared down for a moment at the stool Troy was sitting on. A name that was written on Troy's piece of furniture, and long admired by him. This was to be a beguiling temperament that rivaled all. For what was a servant to a master but a piece of furniture on display.

"Yes, I do!" Sonja voiced, "Clarkston, Sonja, Jo Clarkston."

Troy glanced at the ottoman and back to his father, "Good, that's good. Well dad, how about it?"

Young Master Branham signed papers showing Sonja to be a free woman. That is so-long-as she stayed on his plantation. A freedom in name-only but to her it was the beginning of a relationship that could be her ticket out of this place.

CHAPTER 19

September 16th, 1861

"Listening is the fabric of relationships, and talks, are the thread from which it is woven. To make a beautiful garment, it takes more fabric than it does thread."

That is to say, it takes more listening than it does talking, and if it is not well sown, it will come apart, at the seems. One should never assume someone's intentions, based on what *seems* to be going on.

If ever, there was one thing Gertie was good at, it was, knowing how to relate. Some nights, she and Sonja would stay up late at night and sit out under the stars, just talking about people and places, and what the world might be like someday, way far off in the future.

Late one night, Troy Branham Jr. crept out to the huts where the women were kept. Ole Mamma Gertie looked up as he entered through the short gateway, apprehension on her face. Sonja was sitting beside her. He realized he had obviously broken into a private conversation. He didn't care; there were more important things on his mind than what the two women might have been discussing.

Branham received a letter that evening. He was to report to his naval ship. As a high-ranking officer in the Navy, his security clearance allowed him to be notified of a new Enrollment Act. Rather than a universal draft, the Confederate Congress was enacting the first mass Conscription on the North American continent.

Even though he had already served his time in the Navy, a Selective Service program was going to be issued and they increased the age limit from thirty-five to forty-five years of age.

"Sonja Jo, you're needed up to the house," he told her.

The girl clasped her small hands over her heart, fear in her eyes. The master looked stern. What on earth had she done to cause such a look to cross his face?

As they walked out of the light of Gertie's lamp, she shook her head and whispered under her breath, "Men love with their eyes, and women love with their ears."

Sonja trembled all the way to the mansion, wishing that the master would give her a hint of her trouble that lay ahead.

Up the back staircase the two went, as if on feathered feet. He led her into his bedroom by her elbow and shut the heavy door.

She felt his expectations for her, and she watched his face as her clothes slid silently to the hardwood floor. He savored this moment with a depth that fell into the early morning light. It would be no telling, possibly a very long time, before he would have a woman again.

Santa Anna, the Mexicans dictator, had attacked the American troops along the southern border of Texas.

"Procurement" as the header of his official government letter wrote.

The next few weeks would find him preparing to head to the southern borders, commanding the USS Cyan, a warship. The ship would leave the port immediately upon his arrival; his ship carrying the guns that the American confederate army would need. But tonight, was his, and he would be in no hurry. Sonja slid silently onto the oversized bed, obediently accepting her master's advances as he slid beside her.

CHAPTER 20

September 17th, 1861

With the early morning, the blunt thunder of boots, thumped all around the upstairs. Everyone heard the impatient footsteps of young Troy throughout the entire estate as he passed about in his Confederate States Marine Corps uniform.

All day he was upstairs getting his things together for the long ride to the coast. As he stood there in front of the full-length window, gazing out across the Blue Mountains, Sonja paused for a moment as she passed by his open bedroom doorway. The shine of his brass buttons caused the evening's sun to gleam into her eyes, with every sway.

She ran in and threw her arms around him. He steadied his scotch, as she breathed deep into his cotton white cravat.

"Easy girl, it's not forever." Troy smiled.

Sonja relaxed her hug, "You will be able to write and let me know how you are?"

"Of Course." Troy reassured, "I will write to you as often as I can, it's only for a few years."

Sonja was placed under the supervision of Mamma Gertie but she was the only other servant besides Mister William to be given a room of her own in The Great House.

Troy and Sonja became very close and exchanged several letters while he was out at sea. All of his correspondences titled 'Instructions for Gertie'. His father never suspected a thing, and ole Mamma Gertie read every letter because poor Sonja, along with most of the others here, could not read.

Few at the plantation knew about their love-affair; falling in love was not looked upon kindly even among the others. Murder was not beneath anyone who thought mixing whites and blacks was an abomination. The Great House was quiet in the absences of Troy Eugene Branham Junior. Of course, no one would even admit to themselves that they liked it that way.

Four long years had passed by and the war had long since closed to an end. In many places they gave the Workhands the right to leave if they so choose to.

By now most of them were very well skilled and had no trouble at all finding fine jobs in town. Of course, none of the town's folk were going to make it easy for any of them. Stricter local rules, like harder spelling tests, if they wanted the eligibility to vote.

If their former masters were a respected member of the community, it was an asset to mention their name when trying to get a job. The first question any store-owner would ask was, "Who did you used to belong to?"

This name eventually became the last name of the black man or woman who was free. For example, instead of calling them 'William of the Branham's he would simply be addressed as Mister William Branham, and everyone who knew the Branham's, understood the man's background.

They forced those who were owned by families that were not thought of very highly in society to find more menial labor and their last names became the field of their chosen profession. One of the hardest jobs in town was a man who worked shoeing horses, called a Smith, and that is why most Smiths in those days were usually black because no white man wanted the job.

CHAPTER 21

1869

The mansion overlooked the six shacks and three huts, set on the back of the two-hundred-acre estate, housing the men and women who called the mansion "The Great House". Emma had another name for it, but one that she could not repeat, not even to the lady that oversaw her.

Mamma Gertie had a time raising poor Emma, not that she was a bad child mind you, just outspoken at times. Emma's mother had been the same way. Many a time her mother's mouth got her back-handed right where she stood. An entire day could have gone uneventful, if only she had just bitten her upper-lip.

Gertie often spoke of Emma's mother, "My poor sweet Sonja," she would always say. The life of a child conceived under these circumstances was in danger. For this reason, Emma's wavy hair always had to be trimmed very short. Thelma would sometimes tease that Emma would have made a pretty little boy.

On the far corner of the Branham Plantation, there were six, old, rundown buildings that none of the workers liked. Each building housed between fifteen to twenty men. The leaky ceilings were always in disrepair, and none of them had ever seen a brush of paint.

They forced all one hundred to pile up in these crude ole dwellings at night, and in the summer the heat was impossible to bare.

The only comfort that this Purlieu, as the Branham's referred to them were the elegant cast iron parlor stoves, which more than sufficiently heated these shacks in the coldest of winters. Most of the time, they left the windows and doors open all winter long - just to let out some of the heat.

There were two medium-sized places on top of these wood-burning stoves, which were very good for cooking, heating soups, and supplying them with a means of cleaning themselves with heated-water.

Now, let me tell you; these were no ordinary stoves of these times. They were designed and handmade by Master Charles himself; the first of a long line of items that are still made to this very day.

The Branham's are famous for their craftsmanship. Many of the wealthier landowners also sought the various types of household furniture that they crafted.

Laboring Workhands were skilled in woodcarving, where they worked every day assembling handsome dressers, beautiful hutches, lavish cabinets, and even elegantly handmade wooden chairs.

Their most coveted merchandise is their musical instruments. It always took them a very long time to build, so a Branham Stradivarius or Hammer Dulcimer was a very rare thing to have.

For any Workhand here to possess such skills was a prize of knowledge and the Branham's prided themselves on how well they taught many of them to forge iron and bronze for making the garden and working tools. They then sold the many things that were made here to local shops in the small town of Richmond, Virginia.

Here on the plantation, they also had buildings for Stonecutters. They brought in large slabs of stone from time to time, to be chiseled into gravestones and markers, and the fact that a customer's exquisite marble headpiece was from the Branham plantation was the respect for a person's family member, and this reflected the fact.

CHAPTER 22

April 30th, 1869

This was a new time for Emma and our people – they called them sharecroppers now. There was a time when she could have seen one hundred or more working in the fields, now there were only fifty hands living here. The women were given a hut to share. Mary and her daughter Josephet lived in the third hut. Francine and her daughter Thelma lived next door and Emma shared a hut with Gertie in the very first one.

"Miss Lola, ma'am was just as sweet as molasses," Emma would always say.

She often thought she had a face like freshly baked bread. Coming from her that comment was from the mind of a child, however strange a statement it may sound to an adult, an honest observation and not intended to be an insult.

If ever there was a soul that could catch the sunshine and leave it in your smile, it was a kiss on the cheek from Miss Lola. Out of all the Branham family members, she was the only one who seemed to always know just the right things to say.

Lola could look deep into a person's heart no matter how hard they tried to hide their feelings. She could see the writing on one's own soul.

Today, in a vacant building, Miss Lola decided that some of the second generation, who worked at the Main House will meet here and have a school lesson about anything that is darkening our minds as a resident in this new world like speaking the English language and learn a few things about history and anything else she could enlighten us on.

Because the Branham's were furniture makers, her class was fortunate enough to have the room fully furnished with eighteen solid oak chairs. For maximum efficiency and comfort, she had us arrange them in three rows of six, with a three-foot walk-space down the middle. Two very large oak tables sat on each side of the rows; this is where coffee cups and books are placed.

The building had no windows, so for reading, each table had three oil lanterns. On the wall was a very large oil painting. Within the elegant wooden frame was a map of the entire world, painted by Lola herself.

She had wonderful stories to tell and when she talked about how they confronted the Indians everyone there kept referring to them as the red people, and everyone loved Miss Lola's stories. When she spoke of the Chinese who traded materials with the French, everyone recognized them as the yellow people.

There was another young girl named Thelma working here. They brought her to the plantation along with Francine when Thelma was only a toddler. Being six years older than Emma, the two of them rarely spent any time together except during class.

Because she was older, they gave Thelma more responsibilities and work was mostly in the kitchen. Once a week they got to sit together and wear fine clothes and perfume. Emma always enjoyed Class-Day because it gave her the opportunity to look nice -like white folk.

English always came easy to Emma since that was the only language that Miss Lola ever spoke around her; however, learning from Gertie was sometimes difficult. The old woman's ghost stories are paved with good intentions, but that woman could never learn how to pronounce anything correctly.

Lola blamed that on her late husband Charles. He was a Kentucky man and had a terrible accent. In fact, all the first-generation workers here had the misfortune of being taught to speak English by Master Charles.

Now Class Day was not an ordinary day, set aside by Miss Lola. She started holding these classes on May the first eighteen sixty-five. This all started when she read an article in the local Star Newsletter. In Charleston, South Carolina, former slaves were honoring two-hundred and seven dead Union Soldiers. Confederates buried them in a mass grave in a prison camp.

In gratitude for fighting for their freedom, these free men and woman worked for two weeks to give all the Soldiers a proper burial. They then held a parade of ten thousand people led by two thousand black children where they marched, sang, and celebrated. This one article was such a moving story that Lola set up 'Class Day' to help everyone remember where we came from and how we came to be free Americans living in the New World.

This day always started with prayer and asking for forgiveness. Next, we sang two songs and learned one new one. After that we had a grammar lesson. Lastly and Emma's favorite was Story Time.

Emma had a powerful imagination and when Lola told them about the adventures of her younger days, exploring faraway exotic countries, this fueled Emma's mind with knowledge she didn't know she could possess.

Even though Lola herself spoke with a slight Irish accent, she knew several words of many languages and included them in all of her dialogue.

Oliva spoke up, "Everyone, have a seat now and let's get started. Now today we are going to talk about how you came to be here?"

Thelma blurted, "In a boat from Africa."

After a pause, William spoke up, "You bought us at the town auction Miss Lola!"

William is a very intelligent young man of nineteen. His primary job is tending to all the needs that Miss Lola required. Be it helping her to get up and down the stairs, fetching her shawl when she feels too cold, making sure she forgets nothing and if Lola tires of the way things look, occasionally she has had him move furniture, rearrange pictures on the wall, and even run and get her a fresh glass of water from the wellspring.

"No Thelma." Lola corrected, "Before your parents came here, they were all prisoners of war in their own country of Africa. Their government sold criminals -called indentured servants to the Dutch and the Spanish, to work out their sentences and we purchased their services so they could serve out their prison sentence *here* working for us. Your own people sold you to us."

William whispered, "So I'm a slave because I'm black?"

Being the only boy who worked at the Great House he sometimes felt a little intimidated, but his loyalty to the Branham family had never gone questioned or challenged.

Lola informed, "They weren't called slaves until London Capitalists, offered to be paid by the African Government, to help them get rid of their enemies."

William sat up in his seat, as Lola pointed to various places on her map with a long wooden rod, "This massive shift of power changed the African population and eventually was their downfall when Britain and France took over."

Lola could see, this information was overwhelming for William to accept, and she turned and sat down beside him.

The old woman sighed, "I've got some news for you, young man; You're *not* black. -You are brown."

William argued, "What about the Fieldhands - they're black!"

Gertie whispered, "You better remember which side your bread is buttered on!"

He would appear to be a little argumentative but the young man knows his place and he always made sure everybody else knew that as well.

Lola waited for the mild laughter from everyone to calm down before she continued, "Nope; they have just been out in the sun too long."

She said with a smile, "So, if I stay out in the sun too long, can I be black as well?"

William voiced, "No, ma'am, you can't."

Gertie corrected, "Well then, neither can you."

On mere principal William never lied and if he ever caught anyone else lying, he would call-them-out on it and never let them forget it -ever. He also knew his place with Gertie, who has had to put him in his, more than once.

Lola continued, "Indians aren't really red, they are a reddish shade of brown and the Chinese they aren't really yellow, they are just a yellowish shade of brown. Also, William, I'm not really white, I'm Caucasian, and that is like a light manila, which is a very light shade of brown."

"In fact!" She insisted, "Everyone is brown, in one shade or another."

She motioned for everyone to gather around her as she opened the book she was holding, "Children, It's story time!" She motioned with a wave, "Thelma, Emma come over here and sit next to me!"

She straightened her long flowered looking dress and waited for everyone to get settled down around her.

For some people, the grammar-part of class was difficult, for others it was singing in front of many people, but everyone loved story time. The only thing that was required of you was to pay attention because she just might ask questions later.

CHAPTER 23

May 3rd, 1869

Early one morning while Emma and Thelma were helping Gertie sweep the back porch of the mansion, there was a bustle in the hedgerow.

Gertie informed them, "Don't be alarmed child it's just the spirits shaking the cobwebs away for spring."

As suspicious as Emma was, her curiosity was even stronger, and quietly stepped over and peered into the branches of the hedge. There, she saw a small mother-bird sitting on a nest.

With a shocking flutter, the bird flew away and in the nest were two tiny blue eggs and a baby bird.

Every afternoon Emma would take a moment from her busy day to check in on the baby and its mother. Eventually, she realized the two other eggs never hatched.

As the days went by, she later saw the mother, hard at work hopping around the yard, teaching the baby bird all about how to find food and how to hide from dangers.

-One afternoon.

As she and Thelma laid there on the woodpile, she saw the father bird soaring high above them.

Emma gazed, "How amazing it would be to fly and to look down on the tops of the trees."

The master's pet started barking and the two girls ran to see what the commotion was all about. Marley had a baby bird cornered. The baby was yelling for its parents.

Suddenly, the father bird swooped in from above and pooped all over the dog's head. The little bird's parents kept swooping in, trying to run the animal off.

Emma ran over, "Oh! Come on you big ole thing!" She grunted with a tug on the dog's leash.

She tied him back on his post and gently kneeled down and the little bird hopped right into her cupped hands, "You must be the same baby I saw in the nest."

-Later, at Gerties hut.

Gertie chuckled so hard when the two girls told her about Marley's -new look.

"Now child." Gertie informed, "Once a baby bird smells like a human, the mother and father bird will have nothing to do with it again. Emma would have to be its new mother now."

"Whatcha gonna name him?" Thelma asked.

Emma held the little bird to her face, "I'm going to name you Bernard!"

Thelma stepped back, "Where'd you get a name like that?"

Emma smiled, "Because he was found by a Saint Bernard!" and the two laughed out loud.

Every afternoon, Emma and Thelma scoured the creek turning over every rock and dead log they could find.

"I found a good one!" Emma held up a long nightcrawler.

Thelma squirmed, "Just put it in!" She held out a metal can.

Directly, after supper they took turns standing on the back porch of the Great House and tossed the baby bird into the air. It flapped its tiny wings as hard as it could, all the way to the ground.

"It's my turn next!" Thelma insisted.

Miss Lola and Gertie sat on the back porch with them, sipping on a cup of warm herbal tea. Which consisted of Miss Lola's own secret recipe, a concoction of a slice of ginger, lemon grass, crushed garlic and Guabino leaves imported all the way from the Philippine islands. Her bushy white hair gently moved in the afternoon breeze. Her blue eyes, dimmed with age.

She sat there in her grey and white pin-stripe hoop skirt and all black cotton blouse. She always wore her black stockings because she complained about the chill. She was getting on in years now.

Lola motioned, "William, help me with my shawl."

The young black man rushed over and neatly spread the old woman's, off white knitted shawl around her shoulders. Lola's health failed her on many mornings but today the air was warm, a couple of squirrels were chattering and the birds chirping in the trees.

Lola rambled out loud, "I can still remember when I was about Emma's age, we were all sitting at the supper table and there was someone knocking! When my father returned from the door, he said there was no one there."

Lola paused for a moment to take another sip from her white porcelain cup while Gertie just sat beside her, quietly rocking in the old oak rocking-chair. The warm evenings sitting outside always seemed to be good for Miss Lola and the children were a delight to watch.

Once again Emma stood on the porch and pitched the baby bird into the air and the little bird flapped all the way to the ground.

The old woman continued, "Then, there was a knock at the door again. This time my brother Bruce and I went to the door with my dad. When he opened the door, there was a baby woodpecker!"

Lola smiled, in thought for a while and then continued, "Just standing there knocking at the outside screen door. Of course, Bruce had to go out and try to catch it."

She paused again in thought, "It just sat there and let him pick it up. We kept it and fed it for the longest time; I wonder what ever happened to that little woodpecker." Lola then sat quietly in a gaze until it was time to go inside.

As the daughter of a British Navy man and an Irish Noble, she is now the youngest surviving sibling of three older brothers and sisters. Her mother Erma Branham named her daughter after a tree that grew on her parent's land and Lola's name simply means to stand alone.

As the weeks went on, Bernard could make it farther and farther each time. The diligent exercise comprised five tosses and then a hearty supper of worms and one bug to grow on. After which Emma would place the bird in a tall wooden box at the foot of her bed.

After a few more weeks he was getting older now and learned to expect his daily meal after a good try of aero-planning. He realized when it was time to practice flapping and when Emma tossed him into the air, he soared straight up into the closest tree.

"Oh!" Emma excited, "I'm so proud of you!"

"Wow, did you see that?" Thelma amazed.

As Thelma stood there for a minute, "Wonder, how in the world, we gonna get him down?"

The bird turned around and looked back at Emma, as if to say, "Thank you!" And then turned toward the woods and flew away.

Emma ran, "Oh my gosh, that's so wonderful Bernard!"

No matter how far she followed him he always made it to the next tree, until he was so far out of sight that she couldn't keep up.

"Bernard!" Emma cried out into the forest.

-Late that night.

Emma sadly laid there whimpering, "But momma I loved him with all my heart!"

Gertie sat on the edge of the bed and explained, "Bernard, well, he was a tiny little youngin', much like yourself and now he's all grown up, you, see?"

The little girl cried into her cot, "Why would he do that momma? Didn't he love me too?"

Gertie put her hand on the child's back, "Now, thanks to you and Thelma, he can make a family of his own. Without you he might never have been a man bird at all."

Emma swallowed her tears with a struggling smile, the thought that she had become, mother, was gratifying. Realizing that one day Emma's children will have to leave the nest and become a parent of their own. The comforting idea reassured her that her mother's child was being raised right and one day she might fly from here and find a spouse of her own someday.

CHAPTER 24

February 27th, 1870

No one really knew for sure just how old Miss Lola really was because she told no one, not even her only son Eugene. One morning, without warning, she slipped into a sickness that rendered her unconscious for several days.

When the doctor arrived, he instructed all the house servants to watch her condition day and night. Doctor Michael told Eugene that she was in a *coma* and there was very little he could do for her and that it won't be long before someone in this crisis might pass away.

Eugene kept a silent vigil, standing over her bedside day and night, until a lot of the hands pleaded with him to rest for a while.

"We keep a close eye on her, Master Eugene, cross my heart!"

After several days and his body and mind were weighing down from worry, he decided to rest for just a little while. He sat down with a glass of scotch in his favorite chair. No more than he let his head rest in the high-back chair, then his mind was far away.

-Off in a misty dream.

When he opened his eyes, he was still at the bedside of his mother and an annoying clanging sound was coming from outside.

He insisted to a nearby house servant, "Go outside and stop that confounded banging!"

The young black girl quickly rushed out the door to see where the noise was coming from. For only a moment the sound stopped and then that disturbing clang of tin hitting tin.

His gaze returned to the room, "Gertie, please go outside and put a stop to whoever is making that God awful noise."

With a consoling nod she was off to pursue the origin of the interruption of his mother's otherwise peaceful demise. Immediately the noise stopped but neither of the two women ever came back.

After a few minutes the sound returned and so did Eugene's anger, "Who could *possibly* be so rude? Don't they realize my mother is on her deathbed!"

One of the older house servants pleaded with him, "Master please, you need fresh air, you've been cooped up in this house for days -go rest, if only for a minute." He looked so worn out.

"We'll watch over Miss Lola and we will inform you of any changes." The woman insisted.

He really didn't want to leave his mother's side in fear that he wouldn't be there when she passed away, but felt so tired from staying up all night. He stepped out onto the back porch to put a stop to the racket that was going on outside.

He whispered to himself, "Whoever that is, is going to get a beating they won't forget anytime soon!"

As he walked out into the evening's twilight, he noticed there was no one around except a very young, white boy. His curly blonde hair was dull and wavy. The little child was playing in the dirt with a metal shovel and bucket.

Eugene didn't really feel like it was his responsibility to tend to any of the children around here. That was supposed to be Gertie's job, but she didn't seem to be anywhere around.

"Boy!" He said with every bit of gentleness he could muster, "Boy! Stop that! What are you doing?"

The stocky little child replied, "I'm waiting for my sister," He stood there with his grass-stained overalls and bare feet.

Eugene looked around for any other children who might come up to claim this dusty kid but saw no one around at all. Then his attention returned.

The young boy smiled, "My Mommy sent me to fetch my sister; she told me I had to hold her hand because she doesn't know the way home." His sparkling blue eyes stood out from his overly tanned face.

Eugene questioned with a certain amount of fear in his voice, "What is your name, boy?"

The boy proclaimed with a dirty smile, "You know me!"

Upon hearing that, Eugene awoke from his chilling nightmare. Shivers going up and down his legs.

The startling sound of Gertie's voice yelling from the other room, "Master Sir! Master Eugene! Come quick its Miss Lola!"

At his age bolting from the chair was not an option but a close second attempt and he was scuffling through the hall with cane in hand.

As he made his way around the corner, he could hear raised voices and a confusing commotion. The house servants were all talking at once. He couldn't figure out what they were all saying, but his imagination sent him to the edge of his worst fears.

Had he lost the opportunity to be by his mother's side when she needed him the most? Was she really leaving her only son behind, when he needed her most? His next intention was to scold the one who insisted he leave her side.

To his surprise she was awake and sitting up in her bed. She had all the awareness of someone who had just awakened from a good nights' rest.

"Son, come here!" Lola insisted, "I feel I know I'm not going to die because I'm waiting for someone!"

"What do you mean?" Eugene questioned.

The old woman insisted, "I know it in my bones!"

Eugene held her hands, "Help me to understand."

"I can't explain it!" The old woman said with excitement, "But I know it was a young child. My soul will not leave this world until that child visits me."

Late up into the night, she had Eugene making a list of every relative she could think of, every family member who might have young children. She wanted to see them all before she passed away.

Eugene attempted to complete the list of grandkids that his mother wanted him to make but he felt in his heart; He knew the child she was waiting for. The one who would come and take her by the hand and walk her home. Walk with her to that mansion in the sky. It was none other than a ghost! The spirit of Lola's late brother Bruce. That strange child he remembered from his dream.

CHAPTER 25

February 28th, 1870

There was a mild winter that year, and it finally warmed up a little, and early the next morning the sun was finally shining through the burgundy silk curtains.

"Gertie!" Lola called from her bed.

A loud resounding, "Gertie!" Lola called again.

Directly, Gertie came into the room and started her morning routine.

Lola spoke, "Sweetie, you have always been dearer to me than my own sisters." The old woman uttered as Gertie opened the curtains to let the sunshine in.

Lola clasped her old wrinkled hands around the woman's arm, "I just want you to know Gertie, I love you, and I know my house will always be taken care of."

Then the old woman did something that broke Gertie down into tears. Miss Lola gently closed her eyes and passed away.

From that day and several days to come, Gertie would stop everything she was doing, just to wipe a tear from her face.

"Ain't never been nobody, like Miss Lola Ma'am, she beat all a soul ever did see!"

Soon the memories of those lasting words engraved a sculpture of grace in Gertie's heart forever.

During this time, Mamma Gertie always wore a smile, and her very words seemed to sing out. The others always said of her, "She couldn't open her mouth lest a song jump out." Gertie was the "out goin'est and the out doin'est woman a body ever did see." And they all loved her.

However, when Eugene heard about his mother's passing, he realized he came into the room a moment too late; he missed out on the one thing that meant more to him than anything else in the whole world. - To be by his mother's side when she passed away.

Resentment, filled his soul and though he never expressed his feelings, he secretly blamed and hated everyone because they all kept insisting that he should go lay down.

Her last smile and her last words would not be of him. The thought, that in her waning moments, her lasting vision would not be of her only son.

As he sat there, staring down, through teary eyes, at the list of nieces and nephews, he couldn't help but realize how desperately he wanted to be that-child, that she so longed to meet. A moment that he can never gain back and all of his own childhood memories seemed to fade to the bottom of his daily glass of scotch.

CHAPTER 26

May 17th, 1870

IN THE MORNING

Girls are more observant than boys, in a way that a girl will notice things. They not only regard you looking at them; they grasp the *way* you look at them. A girl not only impresses upon, what you're saying, but the *way* you convey it. She will discern more about you, in that first moment you make eye-contact, than one hundred words that will ever come out of your mouth. And once she has perceived these expressions on your face, you only get about twenty words to confer her perceptions, before she draws her conclusion.

Today, Emma noticed old Master Eugene spoke to her differently lately. It wasn't a pleasant way either. She had the strange sensation wash over her. It was a feeling she could well do without if possible.

In her usual routine she peered inside the Study, and to her surprise, there was Master Eugene sitting there in his High-back Windsor club-chair, the crushed red velvet upholstery worn by age. The air was thick with the smell of scotch and foreign cigars.

The grandfather clock that had remained silent for so many years was now ticking. Its alarming tone deafened the room with every tick.

Emma paused, "Master Eugene, sir?" She cleared her throat, "I'm supposed to be cleaning this room about now."

A hard bound book by Harriet E. Wilson lay on the Walnut, Hepplewhite table beside him; its gold lettering drew her eyes to it as she attempted to ignore his presence. Also, on the table was a tall, brown bottle, the word DALMORE written in black letters and had a foul burnt wood smell to it.

Eugene sat there in his usual smoking jacket, white linen all cotton button-up shirt, light-brown knee breeches and white stockings.

He sat tranquilized, staring off as though lost deep in thought. She crept in and slowly began her daily dusting when he reached for her as she was picking papers up from the floor.

A large brass key rested on top of the papers and thumped when it hit the hard wooden floor, she assumed it must be to rewind the clock.

He held tight to her bony little arm and stood her in front of him for a long time, saying nothing. It was uncomfortable. They did not permit her to look at the master sir in the eyes. She wouldn't, even if they allowed it.

He looked at her with a woebegone sigh, and Emma thought, a sigh that spoke of things that sank deep into her soul, he nodded his head. His face, when she dared glance, torn between sadness, anger, disappointment and wonderment.

Emma did not know why; he just stared at her, as if he was looking for something. Almost she could believe that he wasn't looking at her, but through her. It was an eerie feeling.

Then the master sir turned her around slowly, deridingly it seemed. As if this was something he'd contemplated for a long time. With her back to him, he unbuttoned the top of her dress, opening it slightly. For nine long years he had merely suspected, though deep in his heart he had known. But he suddenly needed to know for sure. -Yes, it was there.

Somehow, he knew it would be; the birthmark that was passed down from generation to generation to any person born in the house of Branham. In the small of the back, above the left hip, the birthmark, shaped as a pork-chop. Eugene released her, and she ran out of the room crying for Gertie.

-He threw the scotch down the back of his throat and groaned heavily.

Emma not only bared the scar, given to her from him by a whip, she also possessed the Branham birthmark that represented wealth and ownership of the plantation. Just as he had suspected, she was a child of his son Troy and that meant a bestowed inheritance. Something that he was going to make sure -never happened.

No matter what circumstances that might bare upon your life or what kind of reputation your environment can mark you with, God also has his mark on you. A higher plan, one that no one can take away. A plan that makes you -one of his children.

CHAPTER 27

May 17th, 1870

IN THE EVENING

"We did not inherit the earth from our parents; we are borrowing it from our children."

Today was the greatest day in the whole world because today was Emma's birthday. She was no ordinary child, with her supple light-chocolate skin and sweet round smiling face, this added to the excitement of all our kind. For, it was our belief that Emma was a blessed and protected child of our god Ogun. The masters of the Branham household did not have a clue that today was a secret celebration for all her people.

Gertie and Emma were hard at work in the kitchen preparing for their master's dinner. Gertie was using up, most of the flour and all the eggs quicker than Emma's eyes could believe. Emma wore her usual grime-stained off-white garment and trousers.

Clothing for the workers is very basic, and they only supplied everyone with a limited amount, and these were Emma's cooking clothes.

Emma spoke up, "But Mama, won't there be any to have a cake for my birthday?"

"No, child!" Gertie snapped back, "Those eggs what's left for the master's bread. Now, go finish them plates what you started before you began yammering!"

Gertie's clothes weren't much different from Emma's except for the apron she always wore and Emma always covered her hair with a scarf.

Emma pleaded, "But Mama!"

Gertie snapped back, "If you're wanting a fancy birthday cake, you'd better lay yourself an egg, cause there ain't no more here to be had!"

The old woman wasn't trying to be mean, everyone showed Emma so *much* favoritism, and it was often a concern of Gertie to keep Emma's mind grounded, so that it didn't all go to her head. The daily chores still had to be focused on, and Emma could hardly contain herself.

Gertie ordered, "After you finish them dishes, you can go outside and play, while Master Eugene eats his meal in peace!"

Of course, ole Mamma Gertie kept her cool, to the point of teasing her, pretending to be uninterested in what today was.

Once everything was thoroughly washed, rinsed, dried and put away, Emma sorrowfully headed out the back door. She squinted at the bright warm sunlight as she made her way to the closest shade tree and plopped down.

The day was blithesome overhead, with a deep ocean blue and not a cloud in the sky. It had just warmed up to around seventy degrees and everyone outside was grinning from ear to ear, everyone, that is, except poor little Emma.

Mister Toby was one of the oldest and gentlest of all the workers here. He was one of the first people to be brought to the plantation, along with Gertie and Joseph. They entrusted him with the responsibility of grooming and walking Miss Lola's favorite riding horse.

Of course. Miss Lola was not around to go horseback riding anymore, but ole Toby wasn't much good for anything else and he always made sure he kept her 'Clementine' looking healthy and beautiful at all times. She knew it always made Mister Toby feel especially useful.

As he came sauntering by with the horse close by his side, he stopped beside Emma, "Child! This here day is the most joyest of days to be had, for sure, and you ain't nearly cheerful enough for a youngin' to be having a birthday!"

Emma raised her sorrowful gaze into Toby's eyes, "There won't be no eggs, to make a birthday cake."

Toby glanced over at Mamma Gertie, who was now standing behind the mesh screen of the kitchen door, and then he turned his attention back to the child. The gentle breeze of the day was softly blowing through her raven hair as she slouched down under the old oak tree.

He smiled, "Miss Emma, there's only one sure-fire way, what's to get an egg for a cake, only one way that I know of!"

Emma asked, "What way is that, Toby?"

He sat down beside Emma, "You see that hen there, a way over there beside that water barrel? That! baby girl, is a dag gone egg factory, just waiting to pop out another one!"

The teary-eyed girl wiped her eyes with a smile and stood up, "Now, Mister Toby, how can I get that there hen to lay me an egg?"

Ole Toby used his walking staff to bring himself up to his knees, "Well, hun why don't you just ask her? She might help you, then again, she might not. You never know nothin' til you try!"

Clementine, exuberantly shook her huge head, up and down, as if to be agreeing with him.

With her tears drying on her face, the young girl made her way out across the lush, well-trimmed lawn, but as she approached the little hen, it walked away.

Emma whispered, "Oh please, don't run away Miss Henrietta, I only want an egg."

Mamma Gertie stepped outside, "Slowly child, they're powerfully scared creatures," The woman whispered, "Won't take just any kind of question, it's gonna take the gentlest of whispers just to calm her."

Gertie walked over beside Toby and put her hands on her hips, "Now you know that poor child won't chase down no egg?"

Toby nodded his head, "I know that, and you know that, but Emma ain't cryin' no more and she'll darn near be taking all day before she be known it too!"

As they both stood there trying as hard as they could to hold back a chuckle, Emma was creeping up on the poor little Hen.

Henrietta could not understand why this child was relentlessly following her around. No matter which way she turned or how fast she ran, there this child was, slowly trying to creep up on her.

A couple of hours later Emma had the exhausted, little hen cornered all the way down under the back porch. Emma was lying on her belly because there wasn't enough room under there to do anything else. In the sweetest whisper, the little girl pleaded her case.

The hen was now sitting in a small dip in the dirt that was probably dug there by another hen. The animal sat quietly and appeared to listen intently to Emma's desperation.

"Please, Miss Henrietta, you see it's my birthday today and there ain't no more eggs to make a birthday cake. I know you ain't gotta a care for me none but it would be so wonderful if you could please, oh please, just give me one egg? I promise I'll give you extra corn when it's time for feeding and I'll always make sure nobody takes your pile! -I promise!"

Now Gertie and Toby were sitting in rocking chairs on that back-porch, and they heard every word sweet little Emma promised, just to have a cake for her birthday.

-Mamma Gertie couldn't hold back a tear.

Suddenly Emma appeared, walking up the porch holding three hen eggs in her apron, "Mama you won't believe this but I begged and begged Henrietta for I don't know how long and I think she kind of hugged me!"

Gertie teared up, "Laud girl! What you gone and done, did you sweet talk that poor little hen out of somethin'?"

Gertie's commotion got the attention of everyone who was still cleaning in the kitchen.

Gertie yelled through the open kitchen window, "Josephet?" The old woman came up out of her chair like a spry young girl and stormed toward the door.

Gertie spoke with every bit of pride, "I'm gonna have to dirty up one more pan, I gotta bake my Emma her birthday cake!"

With a wink from Josephet, she replied, "If Miss Lola was still here, you'd not be talking like that!"

The raised smiles increased with Gertie's excitement and the wise old woman shooed everyone through the doorway.

Now, hanging in the kitchen from a nail on the wall is a Hornback, with some basic cooking ingredients. A Hornback is printed text mounted on a wooden board and covered with a protective coating of translucent animal oil.

There is a very special place on the wall next to the Hornback that was for the most special of occasions. A small wooden rack hung here, with twenty-four holders. This is where the eggs are placed when they are preparing the meals.

-Emma carefully placed each one, making it a grand total of three.

Eight long years ago, on this very day, Eugene's youngest child Angela died. He sat in his study, grieving heavily. Death wasn't something he got over lightly and once again, the weight of his depression and anger sank deep into his soul.

Meanwhile, a crowd of excited women were busy in the kitchen. Just then, Master Eugene got up out of his nearby easy-chair to see what the commotion was all about. He stood in the doorway as the women paced back and forth.

A younger Kitchenhand voiced, "I'll get the mixing bowl!"

Gertie and the other two women glanced at the Hornback and read aloud.

"A palm of Flour, a fist of spice, a pinch of sugar to make it nice, cup of milk and hold it tight, and two eggs will make it right!"

Gertie ordered, "Josephet! get the flour!"

After washing her hands Gertie bent down, in front of a large three-foot, ceramic crock on the floor. She pulled back a clean white cheesecloth that was covering the milk. Deep in the crock she clasped her hands together tightly and in her cupped hands was milk, now carefully placing it into the bowl of flour that Josephet had placed on the table.

Eugene walked into the room and began to monologue about his days in the Navy when he could peel eight-hundred potatoes and help prepare a meal for four-hundred hungry men.

As he sat his nearly empty glass of scotch down on the table, he went on talking, "Why, I can remember when I was a lad, my K P duties I could last anywhere from fourteen to a hundred days out at sea!"

Not one of them was paying a bit of attention to a word he was saying as they went about their business, "Oh! You ladies have probably never heard of K P duty; it stands for Kitchen Police and they are the junior U.S. enlisted military personnel!"

As he swung by the wall, the tail of his smoking jacket knocked an egg from its holder. Without even a second glance, he went back to talking, "You know, in the military, the word police actually means 'to clean' or to restore to order."

Emma loudly interrupted, "Laud sakes, my poor egg! What have you done!"

With a confused stare from Eugene, he quickly back-handed the child off her feet. Gertie stepped between them both, "Francine! Take this child outside and wallop her a goodin'!" and jerked Emma up from the floor.

Francine insisted, "Don't you worry none, Master Eugene, I'll discipline this sassy little mouth, but good! You won't see her any more today - I promise!"

Eugene stood there in a confused silence, with a startled frown on his face; when he realized he just lost his train of thought. In a self-absorbed turn, he quickly picked up his glass of scotch and walked out of the room.

CHAPTER 28

Outside in the dark, Francine led Emma by the arm. Down the cobblestone pathway to the row of workers shacks, "Child, what am I gonna do with you, don't you ever know when to keep your mouth shut?"

Emma surprised, "But, Miss Fran, he just kept going on and on, about how great he was and all, if he was really as great as he thinks he is, then can he put my egg back together?"

In the warm summer nights, one could see every magnificent star in the heavens, and tonight was no exception. Fireflies danced in the sparkling silver moonlight. An old barn owl is screeching in the distance, and all the nearby crickets would hush their singing as the two walked by.

The soft shuffle of their leather shoes, on the cobblestone walkway, made Emma think of a song, "I heard a noise inside my house -sing song kitty won't you ki-me-ow!"

It sounded like a squeaky little mouse –"sing song kitty won't you ki-me-ow! -Keemo Kimo"

The two sang as they walked until Emma noticed the slither of the crescent moon high above the trees, "Miss Fran look, the moon kind of looks like a fingernail don't it!" She explained holding her small brown thumb up to the moon. Francine grabbed Emma by the arm and pulled the distracted child into her hut.

-Later that night.

Gertie and Thelma came walking through Francine's door. The tired old woman hugged her neck and thanked her for taking care of sleepy little Emma. It was late, and she quickly collected the child's things and woke her up.

Gertie whispered, "Baby girl, it's time child, let's go." Emma immediately rolled out of the cot and silently slipped into her shoes that were by the door.

In the late-night air, they both dragged their feet until Emma started waking up and chattering as much as a little monkey. Gertie knew it wouldn't be long before she started asking about her birthday cake.

Ole Mamma Gertie looked over at Emma. "Poor child" The master was severe with her. Much more so since Miss Lola had passed away. The child was breaking under the strain of his injustice.

She wished sometimes, with all her might that she could be a white man for the space of an hour so she could give him a piece of her mind.

But no; she couldn't think like that; it would surely seep out into her work or words, and it would be herself behind the woodshed receiving the blows from the master's hand.

Gertie shook her head, "Child; I know you *ain't* been happy, ever since you been old enough to be made use of, up at the Great House."

Emma looked down at the ground and shook her head "no."

-Later, in Gertie's hut.

Gertie sat by the wooden table in her old wooden oak chair, "Well, Mamma Gertie, she has a little something for you. Child, this here be a something I made with all the love and kindness in the whole world!"

Emma patiently sat on the edge of her bed with a grin from ear to ear waiting for Gertie to finish her fanciful spill. After what had happened in the kitchen earlier today, Gertie felt like a big teasing speech was important before presenting her with a cake, "Not just any something, this here be a magical something. This here is gonna bring luck like we never seen before!"

Out from under a wrapped towel, Gertie presented a ten-inch, square metal pan. The aroma of the freshly baked dough filled their hut. The cake didn't have any frosting, and the edges were a little too brown but to Emma it was the most beautiful thing she had ever seen in her whole life.

Emma happily took small bites out of her long-awaited cake, "Oh, Mama, thank you!" savoring every little nibble.

Gertie fussed, "Your eight years old now, child, and I'm expecting you to be more respectful!"

"Yes Mama." Emma nodded.

Gertie continued, "You're a young lady now, and people are gonna see more work out of you!"

"Yes Mama." Emma nodded.

The old woman went on, "You be polite and don't ask if someone knows how to do something, you assume they already know how to do everything!"

"Yes Mama!" Emma nodded.

She didn't mind Gertie's lecture; To Emma, this was still a perfect ending to a perfect day. She placed the remaining handful of cake in the breast pocket of her dress and hung it beside her bed. She wanted to be careful a mouse didn't find it.

CHAPTER 29

May 17th 1870

LATE THAT NIGHT

Not many of the Fieldhands ever really talked to one another and to ask why, is a very broad question. You see, Africa is a continent, not a country. Some of the Africans spoke polish, Russian, Spanish, Czech, Bulgarian, Bosnian, Croatian, Irish Gaelic, and Scottish Gaelic and so on.

The Tradesmen captured people from several parts of the continent, knowing that there would be a very large language barrier. This way, none of them could communicate with each other and form escape plans.

Even in African, there are several languages spoken (not dialects). So, let's take Nigerian, which is where I'm from; the people in the Northern part of the country have a whole different culture, language (Hausa). The same thing goes for those in the South-eastern part of Nigeria (Igbo), not to mention the part that speaks mainly French and other languages, and the whole of Nigeria is only bigger than the state of Texas.

Also note that the continent of Africa as a whole had at least one thousand languages already established before the trade-days. So, all together, the language spoken depends on the number of countries they were captured from, and the number of languages each country spoke.

So, as you might imagine, the Branham family thought there was not a lot of talking going on between the workers. However, they all had one thing in common, and that was ole Mamma Gertie and the simple fact that it was required of everyone who had the privilege of working at the Great House to learn the English language and she taught this to all the others through -storytelling.

It was always late in the evening, when all the work was done. Out behind the servant's quarters, Gertie sat on a one-foot-tall wooden stool, wearing her usual attire, except for her apron, which she only wore during work-time in the kitchen. Now, this was not a time of work, and all the others crowded around her.

In her hands was a five-foot-long wooden pole that she used to push all the wet laundry down. Situated, between her legs was a three-foot-round wooden tub full of water that was used to soak that laundry. The raging bonfire warmed them in the night air and helped to dry out their nearby hanging wet clothes. this surrounded their two-hundred-foot square camp.

Every night they would sit around in a circle, singing and telling stories. Thelma stood nearby in her usual attire, holding hands with one of the metalworkers. All of the women had their own tub. Emma was not expected to do the laundry but she still sat next to Gertie because she loved to hear her stories.

As the big, old woman sat in the circle that night, she couldn't help but remember that her Joseph had often taken center-stage at these nightly gatherings. He had the voice of an angel and was the best story-teller of the bunch. Gertie's favorite was a ghostly story of magic and mystery.

"Once, long ago, not before my time but before your time, there was a young man by the name of Elmore. Now, he wasn't dumb, mind you, just different. Master Charles tried to work with him at the Great House but he couldn't always remember what to do and to be honest, most didn't like working with him. There was just something, not right about that young man.

"So, the master tried working him in the Metal Shop but that poor boy made way too many mistakes and, in the master's opinion, 'He was just way too distracted.'

"Master Charles even tried working him in the fields but most didn't get along with that boy and he worked, well, a lot slower than everybody else, but there was one thing Elmore was good at and that was running. When it was Meal Time, why, that youngin' came running way-ahead of all the other Fieldhands and when the day was done, why, he ran all the way to the shacks and when Master Charles told him to get something, he ran the whole way.

"So, the master *invented* a job, just for him. Every morning, well before sunrise, Elmore was way out there amongst the corn. Running off all the crows that got into the fields. To make the young man more confident, Charles gave him his very own, Government issued Confederate States cap and Elmore wore that thing everywhere he went.

"A lot of us were very proud that he finally found his place. My late husband Joseph, God rest his soul, gave him a machete, and the nickname 'Scarecrow' and he wore that name with every bit of pride.

"No one would see him, all day long, except around Meal Time. For a while, it seemed, he must have been really good at scaring off all them crows because nobody ever seen one. Folks was beginning to wonder just how in the world he was doing it. If anyone asked, he would always say, 'Magic!'

"Now, magic can only be explained as a faith. We all know it, we all do it but somehow that young man managed to take it to a dark-place, and when it came time to harvest the corn, we all understood how."

The woman's eyes as she told the story were frightening enough, now her voice lowered to a raspy whisper.

"In the center of that field was a bloody circle of dead crows and they weren't just dead. They were all hung on their very own little crosses. In the middle of that circle was a bloody scarecrow, made from the clothes of Master Charles's finest! And stabbed in the heart of that thing was that boy's machete. Oh! Master Charles, that man, fear and anger done swept over his face so much that he couldn't even speak.

"The burlap-sack that was used to make that scarecrow was placed over Elmore's head, along with a long thick rope and Master Charles Troy Branham hung that young man in a tree that was not far from our cemetery.

"There he stayed until the birds done picked way his body -clean and the bones fell to the ground. Those bones were buried on that very spot without a stone or a marker.

"As for the rope, it hung there from that day til this, as a reminder to all, that whatever that boy had faith in, was not welcome on this place and if anybody had faith in anything, they better keep it to themselves.

"But that ain't all, one night, just like tonight. When the moon hung in the sky like the head of a fork. Some called it a Wicked Moon. while we were washing our clothes, there he was, just as sure as I'm sittin' here, a standing on the other side of our bonfire!"

As the woman pointed at the flames, Thelma screamed and everybody jumped at the sight. For, across their bonfire stood a hooded figure holding a machete. All the youth jumped up and one ran away. Gertie just sat there as the figure slowly pulled off his hood.

"Mister Jacob!" Emma cried, "I think you scared the pee out of me!" And everyone there let out a nervous laugh of relief.

It was the highlight in everyone's night. When they ran out of songs, and stories to tell, some of the men would make up rhythm tones. Everyone joined in, laughing and having a great time.

They sometimes stayed up late in the night until the cold set in. Even though they were as tired as they may be the next day, each held up his end of the work that the master would have no reason to come searching out their source of entertainment and maybe put a stop to it.

CHAPTER 30

Meanwhile, back in 1985

March 30th, SATURDAY NIGHT

A heavy down-pour rages outside in the night, while the two boys are entertaining Maria at their house. Her parents went out to dinner for the evening and Denise agreed to have a sleepover for the children. It was nine o'clock and they were so bored that they have already played every board-game the two boys own and there didn't seem to be anything good tonight on television.

Artistry is a natural talent in the Glover household and when the weather didn't permit them to play outside, sitting at the kitchen table, drawing pictures was the boy's favorite pastime. It was so miserably cold and wet outside that they were getting cabin-fever.

For those of you who don't know what that is, it's when your mother irritability tells you to clean your room again, just because there's nothing better to do. It's when she restlessly tells you to wash the walls *again* just because there's nothing better to do. They were afraid that at any minute she might tell them to scrub the bathroom floor with a toothbrush.

"Ugh, I'm going crazy." Joseph whispered, "I can't stand another minute, cooped up in the house with mom!"

Joseph sat there in his cotton white tee-shirt and denim blue-jeans. Suddenly he got a bright idea and leaned over to whisper with Maria.

Maria argued under her breath, "No way, we'll get caught!" She sat there in the same jogging suit she had on earlier.

Joseph whispered, "Heat rises! Think about it."

James just shook his head and went back to drawing.

"I'm the smartest kid in the world!" Joseph whispered, "if we go outside, we could all sneak up in the attic. So, everyone would have a place to play and still be warm and out of mom's constant nagging."

The attic is what they called it, but it was nothing more than a five-foot crawl-space that separated the ceiling from the roof of the house.

Joseph kept calling himself a genius, "I'm the smartest kid in the world," Then walked out of the room with a smile.

James was sitting there wearing his brother's navy-blue Gingham Poplin button-front shirt and blue jeans. He sat there drawing a picture of a green field with a creek running across it and sniffling his runny nose.

His mom walked over and touched the back of her hand to his forehead, "Honey, I think you might be getting a fever."

He looked at Maria for a moment, as if to ask, *"Are you sneaking outside?"*

The wind and rain howled and then the two shook their heads and went back to drawing. Their mother was wearing her matching white silk pajamas. She was busy washing dishes while Maria noticed Joseph slipping out the back door with his backpack in hand. He raised his brows twice, and the door eased shut with hardly a sound.

After a few minutes, there was a thump, and Denise stopped what she was doing to listen. "What was that?" She muttered, and a flash of distant lightning momentarily made the lights flicker.

The children sat at the kitchen table trying to play-it-off by making thumping noises with the side of their foot on the leg of the table and asking, "Is that what it sounded like?"

Next, there was a coughing and James started coughing to cover up the noises that were coming from the attic. Their mother was getting suspicious and walked over by the table.

Suddenly, with a brilliant flash of lightning and a roll of thunder, Joseph came falling through the ceiling, right on top of the kitchen table with a bottle of Peach, Schnapps in his hand.

Maria blurted out, "Look, Mom, there's the smartest kid in the world!"

James Shocked, "Hey! that's not cool! We were going to save that, for a special occasion."

Suddenly, James awoke from his strange dream. The clock on the night stand, beside his bed, read two A.M. He laid there for a moment listening to the sound of the rain fall outside. He snuggled the many stuffed animals around him and dozed off -back to sleep.

CHAPTER 31

SUNDAY MORNING

It's Sunday morning and the children are doing what they have always done every Sunday morning since they could remember. They are wearing their Sundays best and sitting together in a church pew.

The Pastor is preaching, "For those of you who remembered last Sunday's sermon, today's message will be titled 'A Moment with God'. Now if you'll open your bibles to

John 1:3. and 2 Peter 3:9

> *All things were made through him, and without him was not anything made that was made, and the Lord is not slack concerning his promises, as some men count slackness; but is long-suffering to us-ward, not willing that any should perish, but that all should have everlasting life."*

When he finished, everyone in the congregation all said, "Amen!" and then sat down in the pews.

"I figured it up," whispered Maria to the other two, "And we were gone for about six and a half hours,"

The Pastor continued talking about God being in control of every step of our lives no matter what the circumstances, and then he read again from his notes.

> *"Every good gift and every perfect gift is from above, and cometh down from the Father of lights, with whom is no variableness, neither shadow of turning. Be strong and of a good courage, fear not."*

James looked at the other two who are now watching the preacher, "So, this means we can still go there -right?"

Joseph glanced at him and then nods his head, "Yea but we probably can't stay there for very long."

Maria nodded her head in agreement, "Somehow the time there might be exponential."

Though none of them seemed to be very good at history, one thing she excelled at was math sciences.

James peeked around his brother at Maria with a puzzled expression, "X, what?"

"Shhh!" Maria's mother exclaimed, "I know, you don't want me to separate you three."

After a moment, Joseph leaned over to his little brother and then whispered, "Exponential, if twenty minutes turns into six hours, then six or seven hours could potentially turn into days!"

Maria nodded again, "Or even *years*, we don't know!"

James nodded his head at the other two - "But this means we can still go there right, right?"

"Shhh!" Maria's mother exclaimed again, "Joseph and James sit over here on the other side of me."

Maria whispered in disagreement, "But, Mom!"

Mrs. Glover sternly insisted, "Hush, Maria!"

They sat quietly while the pastor went on with his message. He explained how God ultimately controlled all things even the ones that seem evil. God allowed Job to be tested, even controlling the devil himself, only to find the man was still faithful in the face of all his tribulation. Then he read from the Bible again.

"For the LORD thy God, he it is that doth go with thee; he will not fail thee, nor forsake thee. Wherefore receive ye one another, as Christ also received us to the glory of God."

And everybody said, "Amen!"

CHAPTER 32

SUNDAY NIGHT

Maria's parents invited the two boys over to spend the night. The children sat on the floor in front of the television set. There fresh, clean peach cheeks shined as they spoke. when their mother learned, they might spend the night, at her brother-in-law's house, she rushed out to the Dollar Store and bought her sons, matching all-white flannel long-sleeve button-up pajamas.

Maria sat Indian-style, wearing her long plush pastel-pink bath robe. Her fresh, clean supple brown cheeks shined as she spoke. Her father sat there in his plush brown leather recliner and sipping at a glass of red wine.

The narrator on the TV show announced, "Welcome to Mutual of Omaha's wild kingdom. The great sea of sawgrass, making up the Florida everglades. Here in the southern portion of that state is one of the wildest primitive marsh-areas remaining in this country."

James turned around, "Uncle Theron, if you went through a time-portal, would it hurt you?"

Theron raised his brow, "Wild animals make you think of time travel?" He sat there in his long, plush all-cotton deep-purple bath robe. His dark brown hair was still wet from taking a bath and slicked back over his ears.

Joseph looked at Maria and then turned to his Uncle Theron, "We were talking about it earlier."

Maria spoke up, "A world, just like ours."

James interrupted, "But different, like going from your backyard, into an open field where there is a creek and a tree and stuff?"

-Theron turned the volume down on the television.

Joseph spoke up, "Yeah and when you came back, would it do anything to you?"

Maria interrupted, "Like, make you older or younger?"

James interrupted, "Make you get sick or die?"

Theron held up the palm of his hands to the children, "Slow down, hold on. One question at a time. Now, just speaking hypothetically, to answer your last question, yes, if you *could* travel to another space or time then you might be subject to diseases that are practically nonexistent here."

"You can?" James asked with alarm.

-The three scooted up around Theron's recliner.

Theron nodded, "If, for example, someone *could* travel from, say, a hundred years ago, to now, then they might catch a disease that we here in nineteen eighty-five are immune to."

James spoke up. "Could you get their diseases too?"

Theron shook his head, "We have vaccines now, that they didn't have a long time ago, it would be more likely that you would just get a minor cold and fever -then get over it."

Maria spoke up, "Would the travel, make things change in age?"

Theron thought for a moment, "I don't think so, but I suppose you could *create* the illusion of age if you kept traveling over and over."

Joseph looked at Maria and back at his uncle, "How do you mean?"

Theron took a sip of his wine, "If you could imagine, that the very end of time is like a single point, and spiraling outward from that moment is an ever-expanding coil of days or even years."

He motioned by holding his wine glass and spiraling his finger from the bottom, around his glass all the way to the top, "Then, imagine if you could jump from one rung of that spinning coil to the one below it, then you might be somewhere in the past."

James interrupted, "Like time travel!"

Theron continued, "Because it's always in motion, if you went back up to your own time then you might come back at a later moment than when you left, but if you went back again, each time, you might be farther and farther back. Things might appear to be newer, each time."

Nelia walked into the room, "It's time for everyone to travel to bed-time." She is wearing a long, plush all-cotton deep-purple bath robe. Her long dark brown hair was still wet from taking a bath and slicked back over her ears.

"Oh mom!" Maria complained. "Can't we stay-up until the Wonderful World of Disney? It's supposed to be the Apple dumplin' Gang!"

"Sige na! Bugsook!" Nelia insisted.

"I don't need a translation for that one." James whispered.

Everyone looked at Theron, "Now young lady, upstairs like your mother told you."

James asked, "But Uncle Theron is it possible for a?"

Theron's loud *snap* of the fingers quickly interrupted the boys' hesitations and James shut his lower jaw.

CHAPTER 33

MONDAY AFTERNOON

The wind is still, and the day is sunny. The children's mothers are at work and their uncle Theron is sitting under an enormous umbrella on the side-porch of his house. He's watching the three children as they play in the semi-empty lot next-door.

Maria stood there in her Pastel-blue polyester blouse, Levi blue-jeans and old dirty Nike tennis-shoes. She is holding a clipboard and a number-two pencil.

"Okay, experiment number eleven, arrow radius!"

Joseph is standing there in an all-cotton black T-shirt with the image of a smiley-face on the breast and the words 'Don't Worry, Be Happy'. His Levi blue-jeans are dirty around the bottoms and so are his Nike tennis-shoes.

"Let me shoot it, James." Joseph insisted.

James is standing there holding a bow and arrows. He is wearing an all-cotton blue t-shirt, Levi blue-jeans and dirty Nike tennis-shoes. He handed joseph the bow and one arrow.

He aimed the bow straight up, pulled the arrow back tight. Joseph held his breath -and released. The arrow swooshed! Straight up, above the trees and then fell. It landed twenty feet away from where he launched the arrow and it stabbed into the ground.

"Okay." Maria spoke up. "That is, east by north-east!"

Joseph and James immediately pace-out their steps, counting out loud, all the way to the landed arrow.

"Twenty-two feet!" James yelled back to Maria.

"Twenty-one feet." Joseph whispered.

James pulled the arrow from the ground and the two boys ran back to Maria.

"Okay, guys." Maria concluded, "On average, the arrow should land between due-east to east by north-east and between twenty to twenty-five feet away."

"So, now can we add the bottle-rockets?" James asked with enthusiasm.

"Now!" Maria agreed, "You can add the bottle-rockets."

Joseph laid last-July's fireworks, masking-tape and scissors on top of the granite slab. He then carefully tapped one bottle-rocket to an arrow. Then, tapped another bottle-rocket, closely near the first one. He wrapped the two wicks around each other. Next, he tapped another bottle-rocket a little lower than the first two and he tightly wrapped the wicks around until all three wicks would light each bottle-rocket one moment later than the last.

James excited, "Perfect!"

Maria smiled, "This is going to be so, cool!"

Joseph and Maria followed James as he carried the bow and specially designed arrow to a three inch by three-inch block of wood that was laid on the ground. This was the launching-pad for their experimental test-flight of their very first inner-atmosphere rocket ship.

James knelt down on one knee, on the block of wood. Joseph cupped one hand around the arrow and used a lighter to light the bottom wick.

-The wick quickly flashed!

Maria excited, "James! Fire it!"

"James! James!" Joseph yelled.

James pulled back on the bow as far as it would go. -Then released!

The arrow flew straight up as the three children watched anxiously. It reached its highest point. right before it descended, the first bottle-rocket SHOT! the arrow straight up into the air with a swift sound.

Resounding cheers from all three children suddenly turned silent as they watched for a moment. Suddenly, the second bottle-rocket SHOT! the arrow straight up even higher into the air.

Again, resounding cheers from all three children suddenly turned silent as they listened for a moment. Suddenly, the third bottle-rocket SHOT! the arrow straight up out of sight.

"I don't see it." James puzzled.

Maria smiled, "I would say, the experiment was a complete success." She put a checkmark on her clipboard.

Joseph shook his head, "It's, gone!"

"Yea." Maria agreed, "Unfortunately, we'll never find that one."

As the three children stood in a circle, staring up into the clouds.

James looked at Maria, "Do you think we can go to the treehouse?"

Maria glanced toward her house, "Not, with my dad watching."

Joseph smiled, "I vote, we do that again!"

Suddenly, the arrow came right down with a loud thud! Right in the middle of where they were standing and stabbed into the block of wood. The shocked children stood there for a moment -in amazement.

"I vote, we never do that again." Maria suggested.

James nodded, "I second *that* motion!"

CHAPTER 34

MONDAY NIGHT

It's later, and the two boys are sneaking downstairs only to find their mother was still watching television. The station announced, "Tonight an exciting conclusion of an NBC world premier Mini Series!"

As they attempted to creep past the couch, their mother made a sound, "Boys what are you doing?"

That question bubbled all of James' silence to the surface and he uttered something he had been dying to tell someone, anyone and now he couldn't resist.

"Mom?" James whispered.

"Mhm." His mother mumbled.

The television program announced, "Last night a mysterious man cast a spell; He calls himself the phantom of the Opera."

The young boy confessed, "We might have traveled into the future."

Joseph mouthed silently, "James! What are you doing!"

"That's nice dear." Denise mumbled in her sleep.

The television program announced, "He remained far below, hidden in the catacombs!"

James stepped closer, "And we're going back again tonight."

Denise spoke, "Okay honey, be sure to bring lots of peanut butter."

"Peanut butter?" Joseph mouthed silently.

The television program announced, "Until an angel's voice lured him to the surface."

"Mom?" James questioned.

"Mhm." Denise mumbled.

"Why do we need peanut butter?" James asked.

The television program announced, "His music filled her with passion."

"In case you get hungry." She explained, "And don't forget your sweater."

James jerked his head toward Joseph and then back at his mother.

"Why do we need to bring a sweater?" James whispered.

The television program announced, "She opened her heart, but another love brought great pain."

"You know, honey." His mother insisted, "The future is cold."

The two boys do everything they can to hold back a giggle as they sneak out the door.

The television program announced, "It was an unbearable tragedy that soon exploded into a tragic end."

-Later, outside.

A warm breeze blows in the quiet night air and all the houses in the neighborhood are dark. The transformer is noisily droning along in the vacant lot. The children are sneaking lumber and nails to the old treehouse. They are all wearing matching blue jeans, white T-shirts and tennis shoes – ready to go to work.

James was trying to catch up as Maria marched in a fast pace with Joseph not far behind.

"Okay guys. Weapons check." Maria ordered.

Maria asked, "Flashlight?"

Joseph answered, "Check."

Maria questioned, "Extra batteries?"

Joseph nodded, "Check."

Maria again, "Hammer?" She raised the tool in her hand, "Check."

"Lunch?" James asked.

Maria raised her other hand with a smile, "Check."

James accidentally bumped into a tree, "Ouch!"

The other two turned, "Quiet, James." The children disappear behind a flash of light.

Sometime later at the treehouse, the children are tearing down some boards while Joseph is nailing new ones in place. He takes a moment to swing the sweaty hair from his face. The afternoon sun beating down on them all.

At the top of the hill, there is a tall two-story homestead. Long brown vines have climbed up its tall crumbling brick walls.

Maria whispered, "Wow, look at that old, run-down house guys." and then spoke aloud, "Was that always there?"

"I don't know," Joseph said as he walked toward Maria, "Let's go check it out."

"No!" Maria warned, "It looks too spooky! Maybe someone lives there."

Joseph shook his head, "It doesn't look like anybody's lived there for years."

James walked around behind Maria and held her hand, "No way! Jose! That place looks haunted."

Maria looked at her wristwatch, "We've been here for about, twenty-four and a half *minutes*, that should be about eight *hours* our time, or about seven A.M." She looked at Joseph, "I think it's time to get back."

CHAPTER 35

TUESDAY AFTERNOON

The utility poles light stood out from the shadows of the empty lot. This is all that is left of this evening's pastel sunset. It's captivating drone of buzzing and humming drowned out any other nearby sounds. The air is fresh and cool, from this afternoon's sprinkle. Rain water, dripped onto the freshly dug mud all around the pole.

Suddenly, Maria bolted out of the side door of her house with a three-foot-long black canvas bag, Joseph and James close behind. The children are still wearing their same work clothes.

Her mother yelled, "Don't you guys wonder around!"

"We won't!" Maria yelled over her shoulder.

Nelia yelled again, "And stay in the lot!"

"We will!" Maria yelled back.

The three made their way around the light pole and all the way to the back of the lot.

Joseph excited, "Can we see the surface of the moon with it?"

"Better!" Maria boasted.

James was especially excited, "Can we see Mars with it?"

Maria carefully unzipped the bag and pulled out a long metallic blue brand-new Steven 150-Power Reflecting Telescope, complete with tripod. She gently squared it on top of the large granite stone.

Maria put her hand on Joseph's shoulders, "Help me up Joe."

The two boys helped Maria stand on top of the slab then she reached for Joseph's hand. The two pulled James up and the two boys watched impatiently as she made several fine adjustments.

James chuckled, "Joe, remember last year we were up here throwing Jumping jacks?"

"Jumping jacks?" Maria questioned.

Joseph shook his head, "They're fireworks, like firecrackers."

James interrupted, "Yea but these spin like a frisbee!"

Joseph chuckled. "James threw one and it went really high and then it came back right at us!"

"Yea!" James interrupted, "We had to jump off of here like a scene in a James Bond movie, it was hilarious!"

Maria smiled, "Okay guys, take a look."

"Can I see first?" James asked and squinted into the viewer of the telescope.

"What do you see James?" Joseph asked.

James squinted harder, "It looks like a sandy ball of dust."

Maria announced, "You are standing on the surface of a planet and staring out of our atmosphere, into deep space and looking at Mars!"

"Cool." James resounded.

Maria noticed the upstairs lights of her house just went dark, "In a few minutes guys, my parents will be in bed."

James quickly glanced at her house and then at Joseph who is waiting patiently for his turn to look through the telescope.

He takes a step back, "Maria, what are we going to do about your telescope?"

"Wow!" Joseph resounded.

Maria nodded, "We can take it with us."

-Moments later.

The three children can barely be seen as they quietly vanish in a green flash that outlined their form.

Nearby the neighbor's cat Sophie seemed to be more curious than afraid and walked up to the spot and sniffed the ground of their muddy footprints.

Suddenly the cat vanished. – No flash, no light, just gone!

Sophie has not always been a domestic pet. She was what you might call, a refugee, abandoned by her former owner and rescued by the good doctor only a few months ago.

James tripped over a short sapling as he made his way to the tree. Joseph is up in the treehouse setting out a packed lunch.

Maria looked out across the hill at the old house, "Hey, guys, didn't that old house have vines and stuff growing up it?"

James nodded his head, "Yeah and the grass was higher."

Maria frowned, "See, I told you somebody lived there."

James shook his head with a mouth full of sandwich, "It's more like, it's getting newer every time we come here."

Joseph looked at Maria, "You think time might be going backwards here?"

"Of course," Maria stood up, "That's why the house looks newer each time! And that four-foot tree James bumped into Monday night, tonight he tripped over it!"

Joseph stood up beside Maria, "Because now it's just a sapling."

"Wow," James held his head in his hands, "This is getting really confusing!"

"But wouldn't that mean we were getting younger?" Maria asked. "We would know it, wouldn't we?" She said as she slowly sat back down.

Joseph asked, "What was it that your dad said, Sunday night?"

Maria shook her head, "As long as we can go back." She whispered to herself, "Everything would be okay. We'd be the same, back home."

At least they didn't seem to be any younger. She shot a glance toward the house. It didn't look as spooky now, not nearly so deserted.

Maria whispered, "Spooky old houses aren't supposed to change."

She knew this because her Grammy had a haunted house in her neighborhood. It hadn't changed in years, and she didn't want this one to change either.

Maria took a drink of her juice, "I think we should wait a couple of days and then come back and see if the house looks any newer -just as an experiment."

James agreed, "I'm good!"

Minutes after the children return to the lot, their neighbors white cat appears behind them -unnoticed.

CHAPTER 36

Meanwhile, back in

MAY 18th 1870

There was a funeral on the plantation. While outside in the orchard, old Master Eugene had just come back from the fields with one of his plowing horses. He turned to shut the big metal gate when the horse became excited over a disturbing big blue fly, when the horse reared up excitedly, fear in its eyes. Desperately, the old man tried to calm her, but in doing so she knocked him down, kicking him in the head as her hoof waved excitedly in the air.

The butler of the mansion, Mister William took it upon himself to write a letter to Master Troy informing him of the havoc that was being wreaked upon this plantation by the absence of his father Eugene.

Frequently, William helped Master Eugene to remember what supplies, needed to be purchased and on some occasions, the master showed him how to read the records-book and even let him write some entries.

As the many years went by, old Master Eugene would sometimes forget entirely to update the books and relied on Mister William more and more.

In fact, Mister William spent so much time with Master Eugene that he had developed the uncanny ability to sound just like his voice and on some rare occasions when the Kitchenhands were standing around lollygagging, he would sneak up behind and bellow out his imitation of the master's voice, "Gertie! Where's my buzz button tea?!" and cause the girls to almost -jump right out of their skin.

Mamma Gertie and Mister William were the only two Households on the plantation who knew how to read and write. So, between the two of them, handling the books and ordering more supplies and seeing to the shipment of the goods too Richmond, the plantation operated like a well-oiled machine.

No one, outside of our little haven in the mountains, had any idea that these two were ordering the granite to be made into gravestones. Ordering the metal and wood to be made into tools, furniture and musical instruments.

All these had to be hauled by wagon to town to be sold in shops. The profits of these sales were then handed over to the Branham plantation where Gertie and William updated the records-book.

-And nobody be none the wiser.

Even before Miss Lola passed away, William had always taken it upon himself, to pick up after anyone who didn't put things in their proper place and his favorite job has always been to greet everyone who stepped foot through the front door.

It was going to take several days for Troy to journey back to Virginia and he sent a letter explaining his return with instructions for the Stonecutters to make a headstone, the furniture builders to construct a coffin and the fieldsmen to dig a spot in the Branham Cemetery.

CHAPTER 37

May 18th 1870

IN THE AFTERNOON

Just on the other side of Emma and Gertie's tiny little hut was a verdantly shaded dirt path that led down by an old bridge. On the other side of this deep stream of creek water was an old stack of lumber. No one ever came back here and it was the one place Emma felt she could hide from the rest of the world. Many a day when her work was done, she would play upon the logs with another little girl, Thelma Lou, six years older and who, Emma realized resentfully, still lived with her own mother. Kind as old Mamma Gertie was, she wasn't really Emma's mom. Emma couldn't remember her own mother.

Though Emma's body was worn from the hard work that was expected of her, she'd never miss her chance to play at the end of their long, tedious day. She was free to imagine other responsibilities. Tall tales of a black explorer woman named Sonja would seep out into their adventurous games of pretend. An explorer that traveled the world over and who would one day, return and rescue her daughter from a life of servitude.

In all of their games Thelma and Emma were traveling companions who would meet in the various exotic places that Lola had told them about in class. Breakfast in Belgium, evening tea at a Café in France and then they would be off to the furthest most reaches of Alaska for a hearty supper at their favorite Tavern called the World's End.

Next the woodpile would become the slope of Mount Everest and at the top would be Emma and Thelma standing next to the explorer Sonja the Great.

In the afternoons when Thelma had too much work to do, Emma would sit quietly and listen to the wind blowing through the trees and think about her mother Sonja.

She thought about her mom a lot; ---a whole lot--- and what her life might be like if she really were here at the plantation. Would her life have been easier, harder, or would it just have been the same? She had heard her own mother was a beautiful woman. Her father wasn't even in the picture.

He could be any of the hands that had been here at the plantation or someone from another plantation; maybe even from another country, as far, as she knew he didn't even exist.

The presence or absence of either a mother or father really made little difference in the course of her life.

-And anyway, "life is, what it is."

It would have been nice, at the end of her long work days, to snuggle up to the warm bosom of her mother, and to be kissed on the cheek at bedtime. Maybe even tell her a story or sing her to sleep.

Mamma Gertie didn't believe in hugging she said, "There was no time for childish fantasy." She wasn't a mean woman; she simply seemed to be an "all-business type of person." But she was always the one the children came to with their heartaches. She had sensible advice and a heart full of love.

Rain or shine, Emma was right here every afternoon and the weather never hindered their grand adventures. That element just added to the fun. That is unless something upset the great god Chango.

When his anger riled, he would roar and howl, and sometimes, if he was especially angry, throw great lightning bolts from the sky.

Emma often thought, "Pity it was that there were so many gods to serve, tip-toeing about to ensure that serving one god wouldn't upset another. How much easier their lives would be if there was only one!"

The great Ogun and Chango had been enemies for as long as anyone could remember. It was said, Ogun was the older brother of Chango and there was a time when he sought the affection of his younger brothers' woman. The relationship between him and this woman provoked the envy of Chango. When he grew up, he took vengeance on Ogun and took *his* lover from him. The two brothers had vied for the envious love of mortal women ever since, with Chango usually coming out the victor.

CHAPTER 38

Meanwhile in the same

AFTERNOON

"The Great and Terrible Day of our Lord."

The Fieldhands were hard at work pulling weeds and getting these marshy grounds ready for the soybean that will be planted here soon.

Far beyond these muddy meadows. Past the groves of honeysuckle that grew along its sides. Leading to the property that belonged to the Branham's was a long dirt road. Most any time of day there was only the sound of song birds and the creek, but today there was a distinct noise in the air that everybody was afraid to hear.

This distant sound, that worried all, was Master Clyde Morgan and his long delivery wagon. Master Morgan only came by once a month but this month we had no master now. everyone feared the worst. What would happen to us, if anyone knew Eugene was dead.

Miss Mary turned to Gertie, "What are we going to do now?" She shook with a nervous tone. "If he finds out the master is gone, there's no telling what he might do!"

Gertie shook her head, "Now, just calm down. He's not going to find out anything, now go fetch Jonathan and Mister Jacob, we gonna need all the help we can get!"

This eighteen-feet long, eleven-feet high and four-feet wide Conestoga wain was Clyde's pride and joy. The seams in the body were caulked with tar to protect it from harsh weather and when crossing rivers. A tough white canvas cover stretched the length of the wagon.

All of it made entirely of wood except for the iron rims around the seven-feet round wooden wheels. Water barrels were built on both sides and a feed box on the back to supply the four Clydesdales with food and drink for their long journeys.

The wagoner gave a long pull on the brake handle stepped down of the lazy board and pulled a red cloth from his shoulder and wiped the sweat from his brow.

He stood there for a moment wearing an all-leather vest over his cotton long-sleeve tied-up white shirt and all leather pants. The weightiness of his hazel eyed gaze, startled everyone he looked at.

A workhand immediately ran over and removed his coarse linen dark-brown hat, "How do you do Master Morgan."

"Fine, fine, Samuel where is Eugene?" The man asked as he whipped the dust from his leather boots.

Immediately several other Workhands rushed over and began unloading the empty crocks that will be filled with milk. The granite stones slabs that will be carved for tomb stones and the many wooden boxes that will be used to carry the musical instruments and metal tools.

The black man bowed his head, "The Master sir, I believe he should be in the field about now."

Clyde snapped, "You know I just came from the fields; Eugene's not there, now go fetch your master for me boy, I haven't got all day!"

Samuel nodded his head, "Yes sir, right away sir!" And immediately he ran toward the house.

CHAPTER 39

Inside the house the black man was met at the kitchen door by Gertie. She was wearing her usual attire and wiping her wet hands with her apron.

"Master Morgan is here, and he wants to see Master Eugene!" Samuel spoke in a nervous exhaustion.

"Yes, yes," Gertie said, still drying her hands. "Of course, he does. Now go in the kitchen and get yourself a drink of water."

The hefty old woman made her way outside and walked toward the wagon holding a tall tin cup of water.

Gertie lowered her head, "How do you do Master Morgan, you must be parched after your long drive?" And handed him the cup.

"Hello miss Gertie, it's always a pleasure to see you. Now, where can I find Eugene?"

Gertie smiled, "Why, thank you, we always look forward to your visit every month. I believe Master Eugene would be in the metal working shop this time a day, I'll fetch him for you."

"Never mind." Clyde insisted, "I'll get him myself."

At the metal-working shop all the Workhands are hard at work crafting metal tools and fastening them to wooden handles. No one looked up as he entered the shack. He stood there for a moment to admire how they all worked with a fascinating rhythm and then turned to walk outside.

"Master Morgan sir." Jacob said as he met him at the doorway, "Please sir, let me take that cup for you. Would you like some more?"

"No! I'm fine" Clyde spoke sternly, "Where can I find Eugene? I realize the man runs like a two-geared steam-plow but he really needs to sign these manifests." He patted a long leather bag at his side.

Jacob looked at the leather bag, "You could give those to me sir and I'll bring them to him."

Clyde shook his head, "That won't be necessary, I have to be present when they're signed, now where is he?"

Jacob looked in the direction of the house, where Gertie was standing and shaking her head and then back at Clyde. The man took it that Eugene must be in the house and handed the black man the tin cup full of water.

The blonde-haired blue-eyed man marched past Gertie and through the front door of the house.

Mary met him at the door, "Master Morgan you must be starving after your long journey, please come into the kitchen and let me get you your favorite, biscuits and gravy!"

The man tipped his dusty leather hat, "Miss Mary, is Eugene about? He has papers to sign."

"Isn't there plenty a time for that?" Mary insisted, "Now, come on into the kitchen and let me fix you a proper meal!"

Just then Samuel removed his hat as he entered the room, "Master Morgan, sir, your wagon is all loaded sir, it's all ready to go!"

"Well then." Clyde spoke with suspicion, "All that is needed now is Eugene's signature on these manifests."

Mary looked at the stairs leading to Eugene's bedroom and Clyde started towards the staircase.

Out of Eugene's bedroom doorway, stepped a shadowy figure. The outline of Eugene's big, bushy hair could be seen as the man at the top of the stairs slowly walked with his cane.

The shadowy figure of a man spoke up, "What seems to be going on down there, don't you people know I'm feeling ill today?"

The mouth of everyone at the bottom of the stairs just dropped open, except for Clyde who was slowly walking up the stairs, "Pardon, pardon sir, it's Clyde Morgan sir. It's the beginning of the month sir and I have another shipment of supplies."

"Yes, of course." Eugene cleared his throat, "Please hand them to the boy there."

Clyde turned to the black man standing beside him, "Are you alright Eugene?" He asked as he took another step.

"No!" Eugene insisted, "I might be very contagious. It's most likely the Cholera that's going around!" He held onto the banister and pointed with his cane, "Just the boy there, give him the papers."

Samuel gently pulled the papers from the puzzled man and rushed them up the stairs where Eugene signed them all and handed them back to the black man. He directly ran back down the stairs and handed them to Clyde.

Clyde slowly walked back down the stairs, "Cholera?" Clyde questioned with concern, "Well!" He spoke, looking at the papers in his hand and then placed them in the leather bag at his side.

"Miss Mary!" Eugene commanded, "See to it that Master Morgan gets a hot meal!"

"No, no." Clyde insisted, "That won't be necessary."

Gertie stepped through the front door, "Are you sure Master Morgan?" She asked with a warm smile, "We have your favorite?"

Samuel spoke up, "Your wagon is ready sir."

"Good, good." Clyde nodded, "I'll just be going now." He looked at Mary, "Cholera, huh?"

"Yes sir." Gertie said, "We've all had it sir, terrible on the lungs, *nasty* stuff."

Clyde tipped his hat, "Good day Master Branham!" He turned around, "Good day everyone."

As the man walked outside into the warming day, everybody exhaled.

Samuel puzzled, "Master Eugene?"

From out of the shadows of the upstairs, stepped Mister William, wearing one of Lola's wigs and holding one of Eugene's canes.

CHAPTER 40

May 18th 1870

IN THE EVENING

Tomorrow is going to be the day of Ogun and all the Fieldhands were singing praises to him. Chango didn't seem to mind these praises, for they had rituals that also lifted him up as well, and not a one among any of them would ever dare take sides.

It was a firm belief that if the gods were pleased with them, then their late master would also be appeased. Everyone's life would be blessed. This was a delicate balance that had to be maintained at all times.

-Late in the evening.

Gertie sat at her small table, impatiently rocking in her rocking chair, "Now, today, a lot of the Fieldhands were talking about a strange white cat! That it was skulking around the stone walls that separated the fields and the Great House!"

All of them in their usual attire of dingy coarse linen cloth and soft leather shoes.

Miss Francine spoke up, "Some people said it was the resurrected spirit of Eugene himself -back from the dead! And one night when I was walking back from the house, it sounded like a distant echo of banging noises!"

Miss Mary was pacing the floor, "You know what I think. You know how those Fieldhands are, they just trying to create alarm amongst the house servants!"

Mister Jacob interrupted, "I heard it too, and there was some kind of strange lights, down by the creek!"

Gertie sat her cup of tea on the table, "Well whatever it was, one thing's for sure, that this thing has got to be the work of Ogun."

"Ogun?" Mary questioned.

Gertie shook her head, "He's the sort of being that would never pass up an opportunity to test the strength and weakness of his followers."

"Mhm." Jacob agreed with a point of his finger.

Mary argued, "Now Gertie, not everyone has seen anything!"

Francine interrupted, "And most didn't really want to!"

Gertie chuckled, "No matter how hard Emma tried, she could never catch a glimpse and her curiosity pounded with jealousy."

Of course, Emma didn't really believe for a minute it could ever be their Master Eugene but she would love to have seen the thing -just one time.

There were no cats on the Branham plantation and not without reason. Cats were believed to be a sign of bad omens and misfortune. It was feared, they could steal a man's soul while he slept.

It's not that Emma has never seen a cat before. She has seen pictures of many animals in Miss Lola's class books. It's just that everyone else who has seen it, all seem to share a common-bond.

Even though it may have only been a bond of being scared, it still made her feel left-out and she so desperately wanted to see -that darn cat.

Late in the evening while Emma was walking down the path, she stepped quietly and listened for any sounds of banging, but she only heard the crickets. She watched every turn, looking for strange lights in the distance. Not that she would really know what a strange light might look like but she was watching none the less.

As she approached her hut, she could hear several people talking to Gertie and the faint smell of Miss Lola's dinner candles. As she opened the door, someone immediately yanked her in by the arm and the door shut with a quick slam!

Miss Mary questioned with a nervous grip, "Child! What you doing walking round outside this late at night? I thought you was helping Mister Albert?"

"I...I was!" Emma replied, "He wanted me to leave before it got too dark!"

Suddenly, there was a distinct, "Squawk." of a rooster coming from somewhere in the hut and Gertie almost jumped out of her shoes.

Emma noticed their table was slightly out of place and Mary quickly pulled it back into its original position. Next, Emma ran her fingers through the many cowry shell necklaces that the two women had been making.

Emma voiced, "There's a loose hen somewhere Mama, I heard it, didn't you?"

Mary snapped, "There's no animals in here child; I don't have any idea what you're talking about, now go fetch me some twine from Mister Jonathan and be quick about it!"

The curious little girl sniffed the air and looked around the room at all the lit candles, "But, you want me to go out now? But Mama it's getting dark out now!"

The two women had no fear for Emma's safety as they shooed her out into the night air with nothing but a lit candle. They believed they had more to fear from the small white specter than she did because Ogun protected Emma and didn't have to worry about the eerie white cat that was lurking about.

Ordinarily, Emma would never believe for a minute in the idea of ghosts or evil spirits, but everyone else was so worked up about it. The thought of going to the barn, especially alone made her cringe.

There were no crickets now as she made her way down the path in front of the row of the many shacks.

Suddenly, a twig snapped out in the distance. As she peered out into the darkness, she looked at the windows of all the shacks and realized no one else's candles were burning tonight.

She could not even hear Mister Toby. Most nights he was always up this late making some kind of racket.

Suddenly, a far-off voice whispered out from the dark, "Eemmaa!" She heard this and dropped the candle she was holding.

The girl's eyes grew wider as she stared out into the dark night. Then squatted down by her feet to feel around for the only light source she had.

Then, she thought she saw a shadowy figure of a man with a large headdress but when she turned it was gone. just then a hand grabbed her shoulder and Emma peed in her trousers.

"Sweet Jesus!" Emma let out and fell back into the wet grass.

She did not know where a statement like that came from, and it surprised her that it was even in her at all. She had never staked claim to any deity of any kind before.

"It's me - Thelma." A voice quickly whispered in the dark.

Emma sighed in disgust, "What are you trying to do, kill me right over? Now help me up, I lost my candle!"

A *snap* from under Thelma's shoe told them both, where her candle was. Emma put the pieces in her side blouse pocket, and Thelma helped her up.

Emma frustrated, "Why was you calling me so spooky like that?"

Thelma shrugged her shoulders, "I didn't call your name."

Emma questioned, with a bit of Mary's tone in her voice. "Well! What are you doing sneaking around like that? Aren't you afraid Master Eugene might jump outta nowhere, at any moment?"

Thelma spoke with a shivering whisper, "Momma sent me to get some iron chains from Mister Jonathan. She said that it will help ward off evil spirits that might try to get into our hut."

As the two made their way down the darkened cobblestone walkway, Emma noticed there was no moon out tonight and it made the walk to the end of the path a difficult one. They could now see the light from a lantern in the Stonecutters hut and hurriedly raced for its door.

"Do you smell that?" Thelma asked.

A pungent, earthy, musk smell with a hint of mint filled their nostrils as they swung open the heavy wooden door. Dying green bushes lined the dirt floor all along the bottom of the walls. The freshly uprooted plants also hung from nails on the rafters over their heads.

Standing in the middle of the room was a magnificent slab of marble and Mister Jonathan was brushing the two-foot-tall stone with a horse brush. When the two girls burst into the small barn, he jumped as though startled but quickly pretended not to be bothered by the girls' interruption.

"What are you doing walking around at this hour?" He asked, "Don't you know there might be things prowling around out there that would have no mercy for two young girls such as yourself?"

"We know!" Emma confessed, "We've been sent for a..." Emma paused on the word.

Thelma interrupted, "My mom wants to know if you got any iron chain, so we can protect our home from -you know who!"

Jonathan looked around the walls and pointed to a six-foot link of chain hanging from a nail, "Well?" He said looking at Emma, "Were you sent here for chain as well?"

"No sir." Emma said, looking at the hanging herbs overhead, "Miss Mary wants me to bring her back, something. I think I forgot." Emma answered and then changed the subject, "Why are all these weeds hanging around?"

"They're not weeds!" He insisted, "It's called 'catnip' and it's what I use to protect myself from Master Eugene's ghost-cat."

"Oh, you don't really believe in all that stuff, do you?" Emma questioned, "Have you really seen that white cat that the fieldsmen are talking about? I don't believe there really is such a thing and Mamma Gertie says they're just making all that up!"

"Yes, I do, child!" He said with a nervous tone, "And Miss Gertie, she be believing it too! That's why, tomorrow night we all asking forgiveness of Ogun! There's gonna be singing of praises and dancing in the spirit and we even having a sacrifice!"

"A sacrifice?" Emma yelled, "We don't have things like that anymore, Miss Lola would have a fit if she knew about all this!"

Jonathan shook his head, "Well Miss Lola ain't with us no more and neither is our Master Eugene! We gotta do something to protect ourselves. Tomorrow is Ogun's day, and everybody is expecting you to be the one to make the sacrifice."

This was the first Emma had heard of this but as she thought for a moment, "Gertie did seem to be hiding something."

Emma questioned, "Me! Why me?" Emma jumped back in shock at what he was telling her.

He put his hand on Emma's shoulder, "You the protected one, if anybody should appease Ogun it would be you for sure!"

CHAPTER 41

May 19th 1870

IN THE EVENING

Emma was singled out to lead the ritual because after all, she bore the mark of their god on her back. Despite Gertie's suggestion everyone believed Ogun would be pleased for his own to lead the ceremony. She stood there eating some of her birthday cake in the palm of her hand.

Miss Mary stole one of the master's red roosters for the ritual, Gertie's heart thudding painfully least anyone or anything should find out. They hid the little red animal in the root cellar of her hut. The cellar was not much more than a square hole that was dug lower than the dirt floor, with wooden planks over the hole.

Candles and incense had to be burned to avoid any of Chango's spirits from discovering what they planned to do.

As the other women hurriedly dressed Emma in a black skirt and a green oversized shirt, for this was Ogun's favorite colors. Emma placed what was left of her birthday cake she was eating in the breast pocket. Also, a clean picture of sugar-liquor would especially please him. As the men lit the bonfire that would serve the sacrificial rooster, a rage of wind and rain swept through their camp like an approaching entity.

Everyone reluctantly sang praises to Ogun, despite all the drops of rain that fell around them. Rain was a bad sign for them because it meant Chango was also watching. Meanwhile, Emma stood in the center.

Lightning flashed and hot tears ran down her cheeks at the thought of what will soon be the poor misfortunate fate of this frightened little rooster.

When it came time to recite the incantation, her mind suddenly drew a blank, and she scrambled for her thoughts. She couldn't remember all the words they wanted her to say, so she just started rambling out anything that came to mind:

"Ogun!

Protect us from harm! Sustain us from our foes!

Clear the pathways, Great Warriors, Companions

Swiftly moving, Ogun the unseen

Ogun is visible in the Eternal Forest of Olofi."

Suddenly, a magnificent hand of light and fire swept over their heads. Emma screamed out bloody-murder at the loud crackling strike of lightning, while diving under the safety of her people's legs.

The fallen tree now in flames and everyone there dumbfounded at the sight. To Gertie it seemed now that it was Chango who claimed Emma as his own and this did not, please him.

Gertie whispered, "This child should not be killing anything - especially sacrificing animals in a ritual."

Mamma Gertie's heart contracted painfully, "What have we brought upon this child?"

Then Gertie had another thought. It was such a thought that for a minute she couldn't breathe.

175

"We brought the wrath of Chango upon us all." She thought. There had to be something she could do that would please them both, "but what?"

The poor frightened little girl came climbing out from under their legs and to everyone's surprise; she had anger in her eyes, a look that even made ole Mamma Gertie step back at the child's sudden lack of fear.

Emma was indeed afraid of Chango, but fear quickly turned to rage as she saw the destruction of the burning great oak crashing down through the little hut, she lived in.

Emma shook her small dark fist to the sky, angrily, "You almost killed me! I demand to know what I did to piss you off? I work my poor fingers to the bone." She yelled and screamed until she aroused the attention of ole Mamma Gertie.

Now, the old woman knew, and feared for her charge. Emma carried the mark of Ogun upon her body, and Chango was obviously angry. She believed he indeed sought revenge on the child.

The old woman's eyes widened in fear as she placed her wrinkled old hand upon her heart, and Emma thought she was going to have a heart-attack right here and now. The old woman charged toward Emma.

Gertie babbling helplessly, "Great Gods, I'm begging you, show this girl mercy! After all, she is just a child."

Then she did something she had never done before; that old woman backhanded Emma right in her sassy little mouth.

"Child, oh Child; bless my soul; you beat all a body ever did see, a shaking your sassy Lil' fist at the great Chango; don't you *never* do it no more! Why, Child, if he wanted you dead, you'd be dead! He's just trying to get your attention."

The old woman looked at the sky, "Child. Land sakes; you scare me half to death!"

Gertie looked at Emma, "Yammering on so, with your yelling and a cussing. What's done come over you anyhow? Ain't, I taught you better than that? Child, well ain't I?"

Great tears welled up in Emma's eyes. She lifted herself up from the muddy ground and raced down the hill, across the bridge and all the way to the back of the woodpile. Her place that hid the evil beatings her poor body had born of one Master Branham 1st. That woodpile that was, oddly enough, her playground, her refuge, and her place of torment.

There was a distant commotion of everybody scrambling around. She could barely hear the men as they were trying to get organized and gather water and begin putting out the fires. Meanwhile, Emma threw herself across the stack of logs and broke down in an exhausting sob of tears. She had no one to turn to, not even Gertie was going to be there for her this time and her heart broke under the strain of everyone's expectations.

-Sometime, later.

The break of the early mornings light, just came up over the distant blue hillside when Emma realized no one ever come out here to get her. Nobody told her to go to bed. When she lifted herself up, she realized, she must have fallen asleep, because the sun was now coming up.

There it was again, that faint aroma of mint. When she raised her head, there about six feet away, sitting quietly, and motionless, was a white cat - just staring at her. The little girl's eyes grew large and fright swept over her face.

A mouse ran down the length of the top of a log and the cat turned for a moment to watch and then back at Emma. An intense moment passed by while the two stared at each other.

Thoughts raced through her head, *"What is it going to do to me? How long had it been sitting there, -watching?"*

Stealthily, the animal slowly started towards her and Emma jumped to her feet. The cat stopped and sniffed the air in her direction. She thought to run, but she couldn't move her feet. Again, the little mouse ran along the pile of wood and the cat turned to watch, then back at Emma.

"Master Eugene?" She whispered.

The cat took a step forward, and Emma took a step back. An icy chill went up both her arms, and a shiver took over her legs. The animal slowly started walking towards her and she kept taking steps back.

"If you really are the ghost of Eugene, I confess to sneaking a biscuit off your plate that morning; Gertie put six and not five, I'm sorry!" She confessed as the animal walked nearer.

Her next step was her last; it had backed her all the way up against a stack of logs. She closed her eyes with a tight squint. She could feel something soft and fuzzy rubbing up against her ankles, when she looked down, she realized the cat desperately wanting someone to pet it and Emma exhaled.

"Why, you're just a cat aren't you?"

She sat down on the ground and the cat climbed up in her lap and purred. Its poor matted fur clumped next to its body and Emma carefully attempted to untangle the poor animal's hair. She realized it was trying to get at the cake that was still in her dress-pocket.

"You eat cake?" She whispered, "Here."

She laid the rest of the birthday cake in her lap and continued brushing her fingers through the animal's stiff fur. Moments later the cake was gone the animal seemed to grow impatient at the young girl's constant attention and leaped from her in pursuit of the mouse on the wood pile.

Within moments, Emma was alone again, and the cat was away. So, she gracefully stood up and brushed the crumbs from her clothes and started back across the bridge that separated the woodpile from the rest of the plantation.

Emma lost her fear of the animal and understood, what superstition was, and how silly everyone was being.

She spoke to herself, "There were no evil-spirits of the late master haunting the plantation. There was no god seeking vengeance against me, and there certainly was nothing to fear at all, but fear itself."

Emma's disenchantment with the whole idea of running around scared of every mystery, seemed very foolish to her now. All of her life, for as long as she could remember, somebody was always disheartening her with a warning. Now she no longer had any notions of entertaining anyone who wanted her to be frightened -for any reason.

CHAPTER 42

May 20th 1870

IN THE AFTERNOON

As Emma now lay safely in Mary's hut, all the other women were working up at the Great House - except Gertie, who stayed with Emma all day. No one came to visit, and no one walked by.

Despite the growing drops of rainfall, spring birds still chirped in the distance. The comfortable patting of water on the old metal roof, cradled Emma away to a far-off memory. The distant thunder rolled by without alarm. Occasionally the breeze would change direction and a cool aroma of fresh lilies and honeysuckle drifted in through the open door. Emma's bed lay opposite the door and she took in a deep breath of the wet evening air.

As the young girl laid there in her usual attire, she had a memory of when Gertie took her up to the Great House to do some cleaning when she was only about three years old. When she looked in an open drawer, her baby hands found the shiny silver handle of a glass picture frame.

Inside was an artist's conception of a beautiful woman, encased in an elegantly molded frame. The fragile glass frame which Emma pointed to and said, "Pretty, pretty." When Mamma Gertie saw what the child had, she attempted to take it from her, but Emma clutched all the more tightly.

Master Eugene stepped in from the hallway and looked to see what commotion was brewing amongst the child and her keeper. The picture slipped from both their hands and when it hit the hard wooden floor, it broke in two. Unbeknown to the child, it was of her own mother. Mamma Gertie picked the child up to administer a spanking, except Master Eugene intervened.

He cared not a whit for the picture that the toddler had destroyed. The word "Sonja" as it read on the back was of no interest to him.

Long ago he remembered glancing at it, and after his son went into the Navy, threw it in a convenient drawer.

But the frame it was in, was scattered into pieces all over the floor, and at that sight, enraged him.

Now he grabbed the excited little toddler from the arms of Gertie and took her out behind the woodpile. He administered such a beating upon her frail little body that she wondered why he hadn't killed her.

"Momma, Momma, help!!" She bellowed. *"Mom-----ma!"*

On the way back, he stopped halfway across the bridge that separated her hut from the stacks of lumber. Suddenly a great temptation came over him. He held her up over the murky water by nothing but her tiny forearms.

"Whining little brat!" He grunted, "How easy it would be to drop you, right now. All you ever do is cry!"

As she struggled, he gave her a shake, "Don't tempt me child! I could do it you know; you have been everything, I might add, except joyful."

Eugene frowned, "My Angelique, was nothing but a joy to me."

Eugene now sat her feet down on the bridge, "You will forget your Momma or the next time this bridge is crossed!"

He shook her by her arms, "I will ensure that you will wish you had not."

Suddenly, Emma raised up in her bed, awakened from her nightmarish dream, her hair and clothes soaked in sweat. Gertie was relaxing in her rocking chair, as she usually did this time in the evening, her attire seemed brighter than usual, almost a shine around her.

-Emma laid her head back down with a sigh.

As the sunset traveled down over the hillside, the rain fell faster and a flash of lightning brought a moment of daylight to the fields outside.

Gertie said with a consoling smile, "It's time to close dim doors! Dis rain's no place for, day-dreaming little girls!"

To Emma, not knowing who her father was, had always secretly broken her heart, so deeply, though she never would show it, not even to Gertie. All the other men in her life seemed to be a grim disenchantment of what a dad could be.

If only she could know who he was, a terrible dad would have been better than no dad at all. Because of this, there was a place in her heart that could never be filled.

CHAPTER 43

May 21st 1870

"You can't judge a book by its cover or a horse by its stripes."

Now, it was not very well known that in the English culture, an 'et' was considered being a smaller version of a larger original.

For example, behind the Great House was a cabin with a dirt floor that housed several sacks of flour, grains, barrels of apples and all the rations for cooking. We stored these things here to keep small critters and insects out of the house.

So, if we needed more sugar in the kitchen, one would simply go outside to the cabin, fill up a small container, bring it into the house and put it in the smaller version of the cabin. -the cabinet.

This morning, like most mornings, Miss Mary and Josephet went out to the Dairy for a bucket of milk. Even though the dairy only had four cows, it was Mister Jacobs job to milk the cows every morning and that the extra milk made its way onto the wagon going to town. We hauled the rest into the house with buckets that are covered with white cheesecloth, this was to make sure the milk didn't spill on the way.

Miss Mary asked, "What are you glaring at Josephet?"

Josephet pointed, "Momma, there's an apple core, there by the cabin."

Mary shook her head, "Oh! Mister Toby should get a wallopin' for leaving Clementine's leftovers a laying around like that."

Josephet raised a brow, "I better pick it up before anybody notices it."

As the two ladies walked closer, they saw another apple and another, like a trail leading to the busy bee house.

That was when Josephet realized, "Mama! The latch on the cabin is broken, and I suspect the thieves are trailing right to that old building!"

Mary shook her head, "Nobody could survive in that swarm, they'd get eaten alive by those bees."

The two dismissed it for a time and continued to the dairy where Mister Jacob was pouring fodder into a feed trough for the cows to eat.

Mary smiled, "Morning Mister Jacob, how do you do?"

Jacob smiled back, "Fine, how do you come on?"

Mary chuckled, "Pretty good, sure as your born!"

Jacob emptied the last of the straw from a large burlap sack into a large metal feed trough that sat up on four legs in the mud.

Josephet interrupted, "There are thieves about Mister Jacob, and they got into the cabin and busted the bolt on the door."

Mary shook her head, "You don't know that and it's probably just raccoons again."

Josephet snapped back, "Raccoons don't trail apple cores to the bee house, they eat the whole thing!"

Mister Jacob flattened the burlap out on top of a waist-high pile of sacks, "What are you two going on about?"

Mary held up her hand, "Josephet thinks there's someone living in that old shack at the end."

Jacob leaned back, "Ain't nothin' alive going in there, not no way, not no how."

Josephet calmed, "Will you Just come and take a look at the cabin?"

As the three arrived on the scene, Jacob examined a two-foot-long piece of wood near the cabin and realized by the wrench marks in the wood it must have been used to pry the bolt to open the door.

He glanced at the two women, "Ain't no critter gonna use tools to get at a door like that."

He looked down the row of worker shacks where he saw three apples, all leading to the old empty building that became home to an enormous swarm of honey bees.

During the day it was not humanly possible to enter through the doorway, but before the sun of the bright morning day, there were two new Fieldhands from another plantation that became living proof that bees do, sleep at night and under the cover of dusty cheesecloth, It was there they found refuge during the day.

Mary looked at him, "If there was, why wouldn't they just sleep in the cabin where there's lots of food to eat?"

Jacob stared at the shack, "I expect they desperate in a powerful way -and don't wanna to be found. We'll leave this to Miss Gertie; She'll know how to handle a matter like this."

-Later, that night in Gertie's hut.

Gertie sat at her small table holding a hot cup of tea, "If they are run-a-ways then we run the risk of being found out and we can't let anybody know what we got here. This is our home and if they learn that our master's gone, I don't even wanna begin to imagine the trouble that this world out there could heap upon our heads like that swarm of mad bees."

Mary placed her hand on Gertie's arm, "But we know they must have come from Whitefield's place, he's an evil man, we just can't let him get his hands on whoever's in that shack. -It just wouldn't be right."

The three women looked to Mister Jacob who was standing by the open doorway, then Gertie asked, "What do you think we should do?"

Jacob stepped in, "Even if we try to help them to see the light, they can't stay here! You know the Whitefield's will be coming here looking for them and we can't let that be! For our Emma, we can't let that be."

The whispering went on through the night until it was decided, whoever it was -would have to go.

It was in the cold of the morning air, when all the bees were out collecting honey. Gertie came walking with a double folded towel and on that linen was a ten-inch by ten-inch metal cooking pan and in that pan was a freshly baked hot apple pie. They thought the aroma of the pie aroused the intruders and they thought they heard a rustling noise in the ole dusty shack and then they thought they heard a murmur.

Mister Jacob wasn't far behind with an all-wooden pitchfork and Josephet was clinging to his shirt.

Gertie started out low and then her humming began to softly grow, "*Hhhmmm, hmm, hmm, hhmm, hhmmmm, round de meadows am a ringing, hmm, hhmm mournful song, while de mocking-bird am singing, Happy as de day am long. Where de ivy am a creeping O'er de grassy mound, Dare old massa is a sleepin', hmm, hmm, cold, cold ground.*"

This was an old familiar tune by Stephen Foster that she hoped would lull, whoever was hiding in the bee shack, to show themselves once and for all.

Suddenly, the old dusty cheesecloth was thrown back. They imagined two black men lying face down there on the dirt floor.

Their unbleached coarse linen torn and their muddy plaid woolen stockings were loosely down around their ankles. One of them only wearing one plain, unblackened, sturdy leather shoe -without buckles and the other was completely barefoot, but to everybody's surprise, there was no one there but four old ceramic jars.

Mamma Gertie stood there with her hands on her hips, "Mister Jacob, I believe Josephet has either got a wild imagination that's gotten us all riled up over nothing or we just getting bamboozled by a unique hare, who is craftier than we are."

Jacob turned to the old woman, "Miss Gertie, how *do you* catch a unique rabbit?"

Gertie turned, "Unique up on'em, Mister Jacob." She patted him on the shoulder and walked out the door.

That same apple pie was placed on an open window sill in the kitchen, and an old hunting dog was chained up underneath. If there is a hungry soul out there in the dark somewhere, they won't be able to get by the keen nose of Marley.

Late that night as Emma was fast asleep. Jacob, Mary and Gertie were outside on the porch keeping a still ear on Marley's wellbeing.

Gertie whispered, "With our master passed away, so long as there is slavery, we free."

Mister Jacob nodded in agreement, "These two are gonna ruin everything."

Miss Mary spoke up, "I can just see them now, getting into the masters wine cabinet and falling around, right in front of the delivery driver!"

Gertie mockingly voiced as what one of them might say, "Please don't hand us over to your master! Please, we one of you, you have to help us!"

Mary sternly voiced as what she might say in response, "You coming here, will get us all a hanging we don't deserve."

"That's right!" Mister Jacob concurred. "You need to be moving on, before you get us all in trouble."

Gertie mockingly voiced in despair as what the other one might say, "If you don't find a way to hide us, we dead, for sure!"

Jacob now depressed, "When we find them, we have no choice but to do away with them ourselves!"

Mary looked at Gertie, "But how can we kill our own in cold blood like that -how?"

Gertie grunted, "In the river, like a sack of kittens, that's how and won't no more to be said about it -never!"

Early the next morning those three are standing outside of the open kitchen window where old Marley is still fast asleep and the pie and pan are both gone.

Inside the kitchen as all the hands were getting the morning meal-time ready, Gertie noticed one medium sized muddy barefoot-print next to the sink. The old woman made her way through the house. There she met up with Mary by the stairway.

Mary mumbled, "A muddy footprint."

As the two women made their way up the stairs, they met up with Thelma who was complaining about cleaning up the mud that was in the hall in front of Master Eugene's bedroom.

Gertie shook her head, "Thelma go down stairs and help in the kitchen!"

"But I'm not a Kitchenhand." Thelma complained.

Gertie grabbed her by the forearm, "Get down stairs like I told you and don't sass me child, I ain't in the mood!"

Mary was holding Gertie by the shirt-tail, "We can't go in there!" And turned to go down stairs, "I'll fetch Mister Jacob."

Gertie grabbed her by the forearm, teeth tight together, "You ain't leavin' me, now just stay close!"

The two women crept into the room and Gertie whispered, "I ain't afraid a those two, I'm gonna flog them just like an ole mother hen!"

There, across the room, the closet was only mostly shut. Gertie looked around and grabbed a shoehorn that was sitting by the bed and approached the closet door.

Gertie grabbed the knob and Mary held her breath. There in the dark, on the floor of the closet was a cold, muddy, naked dark-skinned woman. Her ankles worn and scabbed from being shackled. The poor, frightened, middle-aged woman cried-out in a language neither of them have ever heard before.

CHAPTER 44

May 22nd 1870

"A lit candle is at its darkest when it shines in the sunlight."

With, the arrival of the new master of the house came new rules. Some had difficulty adjusting to doing things differently, then they had been doing for so long.

Miss Fran came to Master Troy and said she was worried that the butler Mister William might be stealing.

She insisted, "Miss Gertie told me so!"

Troy recalled some things coming up missing from time to time. He didn't pay much attention to it. It's a big house and things get misplaced. After all, what would a servant do with money?

Later he left a hundred-dollar note on his desk, near a book. Next, Troy went to William and instructed him to watch the house.

Troy yelled, "Have Mister Samuel hitch up the coach I'm going into town for a while!"

That evening when he returned from town the hundred-dollar note was gone and he laid his father's pistol down on the desk.

Troy yelled, "Miss Fran!" and the young woman came running into the room.

Miss Fran curtsied at his presence, "Yes sir, Master Troy?"

He questioned with his back turned, "Miss Fran, did you happen to see a one-hundred-dollar note laying here on the table? I happen to have misplaced it somewhere?"

She whispered, "Oh Yes Sir, Master Troy I did sir, and I hid it for you sir, I was afraid that Mister William might steal it, remember I told you about that man!"

Troy nodded, "Yes I do remember. Now, where did you put it, Fran?"

She looked all around and pushed several items that were laying there across the table, "I don't know sir, I put it in a book that was laying here on the table, but the book -it's gone!"

He turned, "Are you sure you put it *in* a book?"

"Oh yes sir, Master Troy!" She said with a smile, "I remember for sure, because I put it in between pages sixty-seven and sixty-eight, yes sir, I remember for sure!"

Troy remembered leaving a book on the table, but he didn't really pay much attention to it and couldn't remember which one it was.

She insisted, "Mister William was in here earlier, he had to have done something with it!"

Troy thundered, "Mister William!" and quickly the young man came running.

Mister William stepped into the study, "Yes, sir, Master Troy?"

Troy spoke with an accusing tone, "Miss Fran tells me you were in here earlier and that you might know something about a one hundred-dollar note and a missing book that was here on the table?"

William glanced at the gun on the table and back at Troy, "Sir, I did not see a note on the table but there was a book! When I neatened up your desk, I put it back on the bookshelf!"

"I see," said Troy, as he walked toward the bookshelf. "Can you show me this book?"

William nervously looked over all the many books on the shelf and shook his head, "Sir, I wasn't really paying much attention to what the book looked like, but I believe it might be this one here," he said as he handed him one from the shelf.

Troy quickly opened the book and saw there was no dollar note inside.

William showed doubt in his eyes as he handed the man another book, "I'm sorry Sir, I think it might have been this one instead."

Troy quickly opened the book and saw there was no note inside and dropped it on the floor. He took a random book from the shelf and thumbed through it. With his lips tight together, he then realized who took the one hundred-dollar note. He directly picked up his father's pistol that was lying on the desk. He looked at both of them sternly in the eyes.

"You both have one last chance to tell me where the one-hundred-dollar note is!"

They both pleaded with the man, "They had done nothing with the note." Until Troy quickly raised his pistol and fired directly over the shoulder of the young woman and she collapsed to the floor in fear.

"Please Massa, have mercy sir, I took the note! I took the note! Please Massa!" she screamed.

The explosion of smoke and fire left the moment shockingly quiet for several minutes. Then Troy put the gun back behind the belt of his trousers.

"Sir?" William spoke up, "Sir, how did you know, she was the one lying?"

Troy spoke as they walked out of the room, "Open just about any book, anywhere in the world, and you will *never* see anything, between pages sixty-seven and sixty-eight!"

William opened the book and realized the two pages were one page. With tears still in the woman's eyes and the stink of gunpowder still in the air, Troy left the two and walked outside.

A servant would have no need for the monetary value of a dollar-note unless it was to make someone else look bad in the eyes of the master. Troy's presence was causing some of us to turn against one another. This was a sad sight for William, as he stood there looking at the woman whimpering on the floor, and knelt down to help her up. To him we are *all* family and we need to stick together and Master Troy is family as well.

CHAPTER 45

Troy stood looking in the backfield beside his mother's gravestone and other Branham ancestors. He wished he had someone here beside him. His younger sister's stone was also here. He never really knew her, but he recalled a pressing story his father once told him. That anything she wished for, anything at all was all Eugene wanted for his sweet six-year-old little Angela, and what she wanted more than anything was to have a treehouse of her very own. So, his father had several of the Fieldhands help him build everything just to her specifications.

All of the girl's plans were based on a reoccurring dream she had of playing in a treehouse with other children her age. Unfortunately, she only got to play at that treehouse for one glorious spring afternoon. As she played in the creek nearby, she ended up contracting smallpox and died that same summer. That was nearly sixteen years ago.

Troy's thoughts now turned to his own childhood; times his wise father said or done just the opposite of what he would have done and proved to be a better decision.

The smell of the scale bark hickory took him back to when he and his father sat in this very spot. He recalled one of the many stories his father always told him.

-A tail of the two sons.

"My sons come here; the King ordered." He heard in his father's voice.

Troy remembered looking up into his father's eyes as he told him the story.

"The king was growing sick and weak and knew in his heart that this was his last day on earth. It was not his wish that his children see him in this state so he thought of a quest for them to complete that would keep them busy long enough for him to pass away."

"Why wouldn't he want his children beside him when he died?" little Troy interrupted.

But his father Eugene just winked and continued with his story.

"I only have enough inheritance for one of you my sons, the king said, so I have devised a task, that whoever's horse, is the last one to bring me a loaf of bread, from the local baker in town, will receive this inheritance."

Little Troy smiled as he watched his father's enthusiasm.

"The boys looked at each other with excitement and then raced to the stables, mounted their fastest horse and raced out to the nearby town." Eugene's voice rose as he bounced little Troy on his knee.

"When they arrived, they found the Baker's Shop was closed. They banged on the door until he opened, 'I'm closed,' he insisted. But sir we are the sons of the king, he has quested us to ask for your help!"

"Dad, how long did it take to bake bread in those days?" Troy interrupted again.

"In those days it would take about a half an hour or more and as they waited for the bread to finish, the Baker asked them just exactly what their quest was. Our father told us, '*Whoever's horse, is the last one to return with a loaf of bread, will receive their inheritance!*'"

"Well!" Said the Baker, "Then why are you two in such a hurry, if the king wants the *last one* to return then I would ride as slow as I could - to be last!"

"They had to be the last one back?" The young boy questioned.

"Yes, and when the bread was ready, they talked amongst themselves of how exciting it was to race each other and what a sport it has been. Then an idea came to them that put a grin from ear to ear."

"What? What could they do Dad?" Troy asked with enthusiasm.

"The twin sons climbed *each other's* favorite steed and rode as hard as they could back to the castle, because they each wanted their brothers' horse to be first."

Troy laughed out loud and Eugene continued.

"When the boys returned to the bedside of their father, with bread in hand they discovered he had passed away, and at his side were two sacks of one-hundred gold pieces and two rolled parchments that read."

"It is with our greatest honor

That we bestow upon our son

The gift of one-hundred gold wishes

Use it well."

CHAPTER 46

Ambling now through the house, feeling quite lost and alone, and his realization for the need of someone grew stronger. -He would find Sonja -She could help ease some of the pain. He was too depressed when he first arrived to think of anything but his father but now -where is she?

He saw Gertie cleaning in the kitchen and passed by without comment, strolling through the rest of the house, looking for Sonja. She was nowhere to be found. Maybe she was busy outdoors, though that wasn't likely. As he rounded the corner Troy came face to face with our newly discovered Househand but no one knew what to call her because, she spoke in a language that was not known to us.

He looked into her beautiful brown eyes, "Hello I don't seem to remember you before, what do they call you?"

The lovely woman bowed, holding onto her apron, "Kumusta."

Gertie rushed over, "Oh, she's been with us a long-time sir, but none of us know Chinese speaking, but she's a good hard worker, she darn near run circles round us!"

Troy smiled at her for a moment, "That's because she speaks Bisaya, she's not Chinese, Gertie, she is Filipino. Kumusta gwapa, what is your name?"

The woman blushed, "Nilda" She spoke in a very soft voice.

Nilda stood there in the dingy-white coarse linen dress and plain leather shoes that was given to her by Thelma because she was the only one on the plantation that had a dress small enough for her, which fit nicely on Nilda because she was shapelier than Thelma's young frame.

Troy turned to Gertie, "I need you to find Sonja for me."

"Master Branham, sir," Gertie bowed respectfully, "Sonja ain't with us no more. She been dead for almost nine years now, sir."

He stood stunned for a moment, not knowing what to say. "Sonja was dead?"

It was nothing strange that his father didn't mention it in his letters. He wouldn't have expected his son to have any special interest in a servant girl -living or dead. The war had swayed his attention away from writing to her for so long, he hadn't realized.

He stood looking at the old woman who had been with them for so many years. Would it seem strange to her if he questioned her further? But what difference did that make to her? He had the right of a property owner to know.

Beside Gertie, and working quietly, was a little black child who appeared to be about eight years old. He thought nothing about it, for Gertie was a Nanny to all the children here.

He made his voice impersonal as he asked, "How did she die, Gertie? What happened to her?"

Gertie hung her head low, speaking almost in a whisper. "Master Branham, sir; she pass away, giving birth to this little-one here." She was careful not to let Emma over hear any of the conversation.

He looked down, over at the little child who still quietly polished the wooden chair. Emma felt his eyes upon her, and she looked up at him with a baby's grin. He didn't return his own. He looked down to see if the child resembled him and satisfied that she was the image of her mother.

He left the women standing there and wandered into the study, falling back into his father's high-back leather chair. After a moment Nilda stood at the doorway, "Kumusta Gwapo."

Troy smiled and motioned for her to come into the room and sit down. Gertie peeked around the corner and tried to listen in on their conversation but the two sat in the study and spoke in a language that was unknown to anyone else but them.

They sat quietly together for a moment listening to the distinct ticking of the grandfather clock.

Nilda questioned, "How do you know my language?"

Troy smiled, "Navy, I was stationed in Tacloban for a few years."

Nilda surprised, "Oh! That's not far from my home city in Baybay Leyte."

Once again, they sat quietly together, the distinct ticking of the grandfather clock seemed to add to the awkward moment.

Troy broke the silence, "So! In one week, I have been called from a strenuous war to arrange the funeral of my father, had lost my lover and had been given a baby in return! -A girl at that!"

Nilda spoke up, "Was there now no one to carry on the Branham name because she is a girl? How much stress could a body bear before it collapsed?"

Troy looked into her eyes, "Is it wrong that all I could hope for now was that no one knew the girl belonged to me."

Nilda asked, "Had your father suspected it? He said nothing?"

Troy shook his head, "What was I to do with a girl child?"

He resented her immediately; this child that took away the life of his secretly beloved Sonja.

A man may want many things in life, but none so much as a wife to be proud of, and a son to carry on the family name. Not that he would have accepted a black son any more than he would accept this little girl but now there would not even be a Troy Branham III.

He stood up and left the woman sitting there and went outside.

Gertie was standing by the doorway and even though she never understood a single word they said, she was a wise old woman and she could tell by their tone and body language that these two definitely felt something for each other.

Gertie shook her head, "Well I do declare, Poor Master Troy, that boy wouldn't know true love if it jumped up and kissed him."

CHAPTER 47

May 25th 1870

Gertie's brother was a fine Stonecutter; Troy put him in charge of sculpting the gravestone for their late Master Troy Eugene Branham I. Emma and Gertie swept vigilantly as Jonathan chiseled away at the huge granite slab. It was getting late, and the headstone had to be finished by tomorrow.

Emma voiced, "I wish I was rich, like the Branham's."

Gertie discouraged, "Child, why on earth would you say a thing like that for? With the master passing away an all?"

As her brother worked, he cut in on their conversation, "I know one that wish to be a king, twas an ole Stonecutter you see and everyday he'd hitch he's ole donkey to a cart and walked way up into the mountains, just to find him fine stone for carven."

Jonathan continued to chisel on the large piece of granite as he talked. He seemed to work effortlessly at the slab, knocking away at it, a piece at a time.

"Twernt any old Stonecutter, he be the Kings personal, that he comes to when he be needing something special."

Emma slowed her sweeping as she imagined an old man walking with a donkey and cart up through rocky pathways high up on the side of a mountain.

"Tired as he was, one evening, he sat down under a tree and dosed off to dreaming. He dreamed that he was a huge mountain, that's sitting high and watching the clouds pass beneath him, and what should he see but a tiny Stonecutter sleeping under his tree.

"Then, all of a sudden, he saw, flying high up with those clouds, was a huge bird, and as that bird flew by, he became that there bird, and at the bottom of a mountain, he saw a Stonecutter sleeping under a tree."

Emma's mouth dropped open and she stopped sweeping all together.

"As he flew way out over an ocean, he spied a ship, way down below, and someone standing there a watching him fly over.

"Then, all of a sudden, he was the captain of that ship, standing there looking way up high at a big bird which flew by. Only he wasn't no ordinary Captain, it be the King himself!

"As king, he was taken to his castle, where they told him, what to wear and where to go and how to act and stress, heaped upon his shoulders, so that he just wished he could be a Stonecutter once again -and be free.

"Suddenly, he awoke at his cuttin' shop, sleeping at his work-bench and in walked the real king and asked, 'have you finished what you be making for me today?'

"When the ole man looked down at his work-bench, he had sculpted something in his sleep, he made a small statue of the king, resting under a tree.

"The king was so pleased cause, sleep, was something he rarely got."

When they were finished, Emma noticed a piece of granite on the dirt floor. To her it looked a lot like a little black frog. She showed it to Jonathan, and he looked it over. The two women watched while Jonathan skillfully knocked away at the rough corners on Emma's new pet. After a few more pecks from his chisel, he handed it back to her.

He smiled, "Their girl, now it really be lookin' like a pet frog."

Emma held the piece of stone next to her heart. Gertie held out her hand and prayed over Emma and the smooth granite rock.

Under her heavy breath, "Ogun my God, keep this child in your tears and make this here stone, of our late master, a guardian angel she can hold in her hands!"

Gertie held Emma with both hands, "Now baby you hear me straight, always keep this with you at all times, for it now be a magic stone, a magic rock indeed. Mister Jonathan, he always says that toads are good fortune. They bring protection and the rain. Child, now you listen to ole Mamma Gertie, I ain't very wise, but Jonathan, why; there's not a man among him that can out do him."

Johnathan grinned, "Yes Mam, we be in good hands now. For when I go to chip that tombstone, this here little toad come a-leaping off the edge. Yes Mam, we be having it made now!"

Gertie sat down in front of Emma, "Child, I know you have your troubles. You take this here toad, this here symbol of good fortune and protection, and this toad, he'll see to it, that you be under his protection from this here day on."

CHAPTER 48

Once again, Nilda found Troy pondering to himself in the study. He sat there in his white, all cotton short-sleeve shirt and loose fitted dark brown Knickerbockers. She stood there in the doorway holding a short glass of scotch. A clean white linen towel was over her right forearm. She has worn the same thing she has always worn since she came to live on the Branham plantation, with the promotion of a white wool apron.

She broke the silence, "For you?" She said lifting the glass.

He motioned for her to sit beside him, "You never told me how you came to be so far from home."

She sat the glass on the table beside him and sat down in the small wooden chair near him, "Bad men kidnapped me."

Troy sat up in his chair, "Kidnapped? From where?"

She looked down at the floor, "My father was an ambassador. He brought me with him to China. They attacked the village we were visiting, and they took a lot of us to be sold as slaves, but all of that seems like such a long time ago."

Troy leaned up and sat down next to her, "Oh! I'm so sorry, and your father?"

She looked into his handsome green eyes, "I'm not sure, they may have." She broke down into tears, and he raised up to console her crying.

The poor young woman was too overwhelmed with emotions to bring herself to explain what she feared might have happened to her father.

CHAPTER 49

June 1st 1870

Emma was cleaning for the Master Troy, sir, at the Great House. Now, sitting upon the washstand near her was an ewer. Not just any ewer. The old Master Eugene, God rest his soul, found it in town one day, brought it home, and wrapped it. On the package were instructions for it, "Not to be opened until his son married". It was the master's most cherished possession.

Troy saw no reason now, to keep it wrapped, and he placed the ewer on a table in the hall. There it sat for two weeks now, by the front door, awkwardly out of place. Over and over Emma had been warned to be very careful with the ewer, but to Emma, Master Troy seemed to be a nervous type of man. Emma wasn't a clumsy girl.

At the front door there was a fierce knocking and Troy quickly long-stepped it for the brass doorknob.

Upon opening it, he leaned back, "And what do we have the misfortune of your visit Master Whitefield?"

Mister William quickly rushed for the front door but stopped at the corner to listen in while Emma stood there dusting the stand and ewer.

"Billy?" Emma questioned.

William whispered, "Emma, I told you to never call me that!" Then turned to listen to the men arguing.

Whitefield blasted, "Now see here Mister Troy! I hear tell one of mine might have run here! If you"

Troy interrupted loudly, "That's *Master*, Troy to you Clarence and I don't have any idea what you're talking about!"

Emma whispered, "Why does Master Troy call Whitefield master? He ain't no servant of his?"

Whitefield leaned in loudly, "If you're hiding her in there somewhere, why I'll just!"

"You'll what?" Troy questioned angrily.

William looked down at Emma, "Everyone always calls the head of the household 'Master' It's just respectful. Now open your ears and shut your mouth and go back to dusting."

Emma pondered in a startled stare, "All this time, we always called Eugene master was because he was the head of the household." She whispered to herself.

Whitefield interrupted loudly, "Now if you and your feeble-minded father of yours would just!"

Troy fiercely, "I've had, just about enough, of your ass!"

Emma was still deep in thought when suddenly Troy angrily slammed the door with a loud -BANG!

It startled the young girl and she swung sharply. She upset the stand. The ewer and bowl that sat upon it, came tumbling. Emma tried to catch them, but it was too heavy. It shattered out across the hard wooden floor into many small pieces.

Upon hearing this startling crash, Troy angrily stomped in to the hallway. The visitor at the door was forgotten entirely as they both stood staring unbelievably at the scene. With vengeance the master slammed his glass of scotch down, grabbed the little girl's arm and marched her out to the woodpile.

Emma cried out, fearfully clutching her pet rock inside the pocket of her apron. If anything could save her now, it would have to be the good luck charm; Mister Jonathan made for her just a week ago.

She silently pleaded with the great gods to let the master have mercy on her, silently begging the toad to bring its magic forth quickly and save her. She didn't know Troy, but she knew what kind of man he was. Somehow, she knew this was to be a beating that would make all others, pale in comparison.

-She felt it.

Halfway across the bridge, the pocket on her tattered apron caught upon a rough railing. Emma almost fell with the jerk it caused when the pocket -pulled off.

Trying to save herself, she forgot she was clutching her magic toad. In horror, she heard it 'plunk' -into the murky water below!

-Not even Ogun would smile on her this day.

Behind the woodpile that sat on the plantation for as long as he could remember, the drunk man lost all control. The stress of everything had been too much. The loss of his father, and he blamed this child for the death of his beloved Sonja.

Suddenly, behind the man, a shadowy figure of smoke appeared. His large headdress of an ax -Chango is here.

Troy bore down upon the child's body with all the stress of an entire lifetime. Taking out the years of his own self condemnation on her.

The smokey figure seemed to absorb into Troy as the whip thrashed against the child, over and over. Though she screamed and begged him to stop, he acted as one deaf.

The last thing Emma saw was that white cat, looking for mice on the woodpile, and the last thought that went through her mind was, what Eugene said about, *"When next you cross this bridge, it will be your last!"*

Perhaps, it *was* more than just a cat. Maybe it *was* Eugene, witnessing his promised fate.

Branham raged on and on, like one possessed. All his frustrations came pouring out upon this poor little girl. Finally, the man's energy was spent, and he realized he was exhausted. He looked down upon the woodpile at her still little frame.

The ghostly figure lifted from him like smoke on the water in the morning, and was gone.

He realized it had been a few minutes, she hadn't cried out. Now he knew why. Troy stood with a shock of fright on his face. At the sight of what he had done -Emma was dead.

Troy fell to his knees, wailing out in great tears, clutching her lifeless form in his arms.

He cried, "Out of all the mistakes I could make in my lifetime!"

None are so painful, then the ones that are taken so far, that they cannot be taken back. The only thing in his life that still tied him to Sonja -was now gone.

Mamma Gertie was at the stove, cooking in the kitchen when suddenly she felt a sharp pain in her chest and sat down in the closest chair.

"Child, sweet Child; bless my soul." The old woman spoke with tears in her eyes, "You beat all a body ever did see, Emma always knew a savior always has to die."

CHAPTER 50

The days to follow were a dark and lonely time for all our people. Master Troy had no idea the damage he caused. He has broken what could not be broken and now -hope is broken.

He saw none of that and spent all of his time getting to know the new house servant Nilda. She did not know the horrible travesty he left lying there for someone else to cleanse. The poor child's broken bones and battered body was only for Gertie's eyes -no one else could look upon her lifeless form.

There, in front of Gertie was a forty-five inch long by twenty inch wide and twenty-three-inch-tall steel water tank that is used for livestock.

It was not vengeance that swept-up-inside of that old woman as she gently washed the little girl in one of Mister Jacob's large feed tubs.

The woman had no hatred in her heart as she clothed the nine-year-old in one of Miss Lola's all cotton white linen gowns -tears ran down the old woman's cheeks.

For in her soul was the love she has always had for the boy she raised to be a man and her faith in Ogun to justify all wrong in the world, no matter who's hand it was and her guilt that this might all be her fault. -This could all be the vengeance of Chango.

Now, far away from all the plantation's daily business, way out in the apple orchard Nilda sat on a navy gray sixty-six by eighty-four inch all wool blanket that was spread out on the ground next to a tree.

She was wearing a two-piece pale-yellow spring dress with a pattern of dark gold flowers. The top and skirt are lined with broadcloth fabric. Pleated lace at the collar and closed with red metal buttons. The dress hung on her small frame beautifully.

Beside her, Troy lay on his back with his eyes up at the warm cumulus day. He is wearing his white all cotton linen button-up shirt, red suspenders, checker patterned trousers and brown cloth loafers.

Love was growing strong between these two and she no longer had any requirements as she was no longer a servant of the house. She spent all of her time alone with him and they spoke of their life together and of marriage.

Troy sat there watching how the sunlight made her beautiful long ebony hair seem to gleam with a blue hue. Her lovely, bright brown eyes captivated him as he realized now; she was so much more than a genuinely charming person. Such an uncommonly kind woman with poise and such a strong will. She was also his redeemer. A chance to start a new life, to make amends for everything in his past. -She was his everything.

He sat up, "I have a poem that I wrote before I went into the Navy. I always knew that somehow; I would know who to give this to and I would like to give it to you. Would you accept this as a token of my love and affection?"

"Oh course," she said with a smile.

She unrolled the parchment that he gave to her.

Just suppose a gentle breeze would blow.

Where the sunrise always shines.

And there were fields and grass and time and only me and you.

They say these daydreams are for children.

But my love is a simple thing.

And if all my dreams could come to pass, would you wear my wedding ring?

And then I'd suppose a time, for me and you.

And somehow, I could always know that you were always mine.

Where jealous ears could never hear the love words that we speak.

Then hand in hand we'd face some storms, and we'd turn those skies to blue. And then I'd suppose a place for me and you.

CHAPTER 51

Present Day 1985

April 4th,

THURSDAY AFTERNOON

The day is wet and chilly and a lingering fog made the windy day seem later than it really was but today at the Glover household is the greatest day in the whole world because today is James Michael Glovers ninth birthday. He is blowing out his candles on a dark chocolate cake that looks like the Bat-Signal. This was not an ordinary cake. It wasn't even a very well made one but it was the greatest one ever made because James got to make it himself. He could barely hold back a proud smile every time he glanced its way.

When the boys saw the movie Jaws and everybody was afraid to go back in the water, James was playing with a rubber shark in the bathtub. When they saw the movie Magic and everyone was afraid of puppets, James had a Charlie McCarthy and when they saw the movie Nightmare on Elm Street and everyone was afraid to go back to sleep, James was Freddy Krueger for Halloween. a fearless young man who sleeps with fifteen stuffed animals in his bed.

He stood there wearing his white long-sleeve button-up shirt under blue and white patterned sleeveless sweater and black corduroy slacks.

Aunt Jennifer is sitting in a recliner chair wearing her off-the-shoulder sweatshirt and white shorts. Her husband Jason is sitting on a cushioned footstool at the end of the chair. He is strumming on his favorite acoustic guitar.

He still has on his Barracuda jacket over an off white all cotton short-sleeve shirt and Calvin Klein blue jeans.

Jason never liked using a guitar pick, and he developed a technique of softly brushing the tips of all his fingers against the strings. His charming melody is so soothing, so gentle that everyone hushes for a moment to hear him play. The random finger-picking that he has perfected into an amazing harmony, stirs the imagination of the three children.

He has always been very good with anything that involved using his hands. Jason is thirty-seven years old with short, curly, dark-brown hair and green eyes. An average sized thinly built man with aged hands from working for years as a maintenance manager for a hotel in downtown Richmond.

Unlike the hectic demands of his present career, for the past ten years Jason and his wife Jennifer have been living, way outside of town, on eighty acres of wooded land. Every weekend they have been inviting troubled teens from the local Juvenile Detention Center, to camp-out and have prayer and craft projects to teach them about Jesus.

Most of their camping trips involved inviting the parents of the troubled teens to come and join them but they have never had a parent find the time to attend. The children didn't mind because most of their problems came from the home-life and according to most of them, their parents were the problem.

It's a very bold endeavor to try and enlighten these kids. On a few occasions Jason has had to wrestle one from trying to slit her own wrists; however, each and every weekend, always ended with all of the children hugging each other's necks and rededicating their lives back to Christ.

CHAPTER 51

Maria sat intently on the edge of her seat wearing her all cotton mini dalmatian dot bib skirt with adjustable button suspenders. A bold plaid shirt with short sleeves and white bob socks.

Joseph sat on the couch next to Maria wearing his white all cotton button up collared shirt and Oshkosh blue denim jeans. As his uncle played, his imagination ran wild.

He leaned over and whispered to her, "When I close my eyes, I can imagine a young man sitting under a shade-tree on a hillside and the wind blowing through the trees."

Maria turned to him and smiled in amazement at the ideas of her cousin's creative mind.

James interrupted, "Uncle Jason, do you know a really cool story you could tell us?"

"Yeah!" Maria concurred, "Can we hear one of your stories?"

"Let me think," Jason said as he eased down into the floor.

"Okay." Jason nodded, "This story is called The Storyteller."

The children got comfortable in the floor around their uncle; James went over and sat down in his Uncle Theron's lap while Jason continued with his story.

"Once upon a time, as most good stories begin, there was a young man in a village by the name of Tom. Every day he could be found in the streets, preaching to everyone about the goodness of God. Some people liked to hear him tell stories of King David and Goliath, or the shepherd boy who happened upon a child lying in a manger.

"Tom was a great storyteller. However, when he would start ranting on about how everyone is a sinner and how they are all going to Hell if they don't change their ways.

"Well, everyone in the village would begin arguing with him and try to run him off. In fact, Tom had been arrested for disturbing the peace, on many occasions.

"Now in his defense, Tom was so very knowledgeable about the bible that you could ask him any question and he would have a marvelous answer that would pause, most intellectuals.

"However, his brother Bob, on the other hand, could not tell you anything about the bible at all. Bob was a very knowledgeable young man, as long as you stuck to subjects like geology and history. In fact, Bob was an expert on anything worldly. You could ask him anything about the distance of the sun from the earth, or how long it would take for a sparrow to travel around the world.

"He also had a very peculiar sense of humor, one time as he sat pondering alone someone once asked him, Hey Bob what's a matter?" He quickly replied, *"A red rooted plant with yellow flowers!"* If his brother had not been near to elaborate, no one would have understood that a *Matter* is also the name of a plant.

"Today, just like most days, his brother Tom was walking around the village preaching the promise of everlasting peace, until he got on the subject of hell and eternal damnation. Many of the people were getting angry, and a fight broke out in front of the Bakery Shop.

"Master Hamilton the Shopkeeper came outside with broom in hand and began beating the two men until they stopped fighting. While this was going on, someone brought all of this to the attention of the king who was visiting the local Stonecutter on the next street.

"Everyone except Tom and the young man bowed down to the approaching king.

"'My Lord,' said the Shopkeeper, 'Tom was fighting out in front of my store and I tried to break it up!'

"Suddenly, everyone standing there started voicing their discontentment of putting up with Tom. The king looked over at him. Tom, who was now kneeling in the dirt road, bowed his head.

"The king sternly voiced above the noise, 'I have dealt with you many times Tom, and now everyone wants me to do something about you, once and for all.'

"As the crowd quieted down to a murmur the king continued, 'Tom, in three days you will appear before my court and prove to me that your God exists or I will put you in jail again, but this time I will throw away the key and no one will have to put up with you ever again.

'However, if in three days' time you can prove to me, he does exist, then I will give you a building to preach your word and people can come and listen to you -if they so choose, but you will never be allowed to preach in the streets ever again.'

"Tom was both excited and scared out of his wits. What was he going to do, and what could he possibly say to convince the king's court that there really is a God? Tom ran all the way home and hid under the covers until his brother Bob came home.

"'My brother, I have really done it this time,' said Tom, 'The king is going to put me in jail if I cannot prove to them that God exists!'

"Bob sighed in disbelief, 'They've put you in jail many times before.'

"Tom cried, 'The king himself is going to throw away the key!'

"Bob shook his head and instructed his brother to hide here at home, 'I will go before the king and tell them I am you. I will answer the king's questions; I know how to handle a king.'

"When the three days had come, Bob went up before the court and stood before the king.

"The king sat upon his throne, 'Good morning, Tom, because you claim that your God is, all knowing. I will ask you three questions, and if your God will spare your life, he will give you the answers, but if not, then this key will seal your doom forever.'

"After a slight bow, Bob smiled and looked at the king and said, 'My lord, what is your first question?'

"The king stood and walked around the courtroom with a sheet of paper in hand, reading over it and then looked back at Bob., 'My first question is How deep is the ocean? Some of my scholars have been debating this question for many years and.

"Bob held his open palm at the king and interrupted, 'Oh, that's easy, how deep is the ocean? Why. it's just a stone's-throw away because if you throw the stone into the ocean, it will go all the way to the bottom!'

"There was laughter, from everyone in the courtroom. Even the king chuckled out loud, 'Okay Tom, I will give you that one but my next question is not going to be so easy.'

"After a moment the king continued, 'How many stars are there in the heavens?'

"Bob walked around the room and then looked at the king, 'I know exactly how many stars there are in the heavens, there are one hundred billion, four hundred and sixty million, eight hundred and twenty thousand, four hundred and twelve, and if you don't believe me, you can count them yourself!'

"Again, laughter filled the courtroom, but this time the king was not laughing. He walked up to Bob and looked him in the eyes, 'I have only one more question Tom, and then I will set you free.' After a pause, he continued, 'What am I thinking?'

"Bob took a breath, 'My king, I know exactly what you are thinking.'

"'You do?' exclaimed the king.

"'Yes, my Lord.' Bob explained, 'You think I'm Tom, and I am not, I'm Bob.'

"The king laughed so hard his voice became a little hoarse, Bob jumped on that horse and rode away and was never seen again. As for Tom, to this very day, he can still be found in his building preaching to everyone who will come inside and listen, but he will never preach in the streets for the king will have his head."

Mrs. Glover cleared her throat, "Come on everybody, it's time for James to open his gifts."

"The end," Jason commented as he climbed back up on the foot stool.

Joseph and Maria immediately jumped up. The house is beginning to get noisy again, and everyone is in the dining room, looking for a place to watch James open his presents.

James looked over at Theron, "Uncle Theron, are you still in the Navy? If I went to work with you sometime, could I help drive the ship? It seems like it would be very easy to drive. You're out in the middle of the ocean, what could you bump into?"

Joseph interrupted his rambling, "Uncle Jason, have you seen the new Indiana Jones movie? It was really awesome!"

Jennifer spoke up, "Yes, we saw it last summer, it was very action packed, James, are you still into Batman?"

Maria chuckled, "Oh yes, he's totally into Batman!"

Mrs. Glover handed James the first present on the table and he tears into it like its Christmas morning, "James, you first have to read who it's from."

He looked at the remains of the wrappings and realized it was from Uncle Jason and Aunt Jennifer, "A Davy Crockett pocket-knife!" James excited.

Denise widened her eyes at Jason but he never glanced in her direction. She started to disapprove and walked back into the kitchen.

Theron insisted, "Now you have to open mine next."

Maria fumbled through the gifts and hands James one marked, *"To James from Uncle Theron and Aunt Nelia."*

Like all the other gifts, he dug into it like a boy gone wild. The first thing he saw was a big black cloth and his first reaction was, "Oh no, not clothes!"

As he slowly lifted it out of the box, his smile got wider, "A brand new Batman cape!"

Nelia came out of the kitchen wearing her slim, forest-green knee-high dress and black high-heel shoes. She was holding two paper plates with cake and ice cream and handed one of them to her husband.

James thanked both of them with a big hug, and with no inhibitions whatsoever, he ran to his mother so she could help him put it on. The rest of the gift opening went along with a lot more pride as James sported about in his long black cape.

Maria smiled, "There'll be no living with him now."

Denise handed Maria and James a paper plate with cake and ice cream.

"Salamat, po!" Maria exclaimed.

"What does that mean?" James asked.

"Thank you." Maria explained.

James took a bite of cake, "Salamat po, mom!" He exclaimed.

His uncles, being fans of adventure, themselves have always indulged the children in expressing their imaginations. if there is any style that the two boys are wearing, it's credited to their uncles. Denise could never afford designer clothes or Star Wars toys and the basket-ball that Joseph is so fond of was also one of the many gifts from their uncles.

"Mhm...Masarap." Maria whispered. James looked at her with questioning eyes.

"That means de'licious!" She said with a smile.

James took another bite of cake, "Ma'sarap! Mom!" He exclaimed.

As Denise handed Joseph a paper plate of cake and ice cream. Jason looked at the children, "So, what have you guys been doing with your time, now that you're out of school?"

James with a huge grin, "We've been building a treehouse!"

Joseph nudged him, "In... In the backyard."

Uncle Jason sat up in his seat, "Oh really, that sounds interesting, may we have a look at it?"

"Oh no, no," Joseph shook his head.

James interrupted, "It's not finished yet."

Maria interrupted the two boys, "Yeah and we don't want anybody to see it until we get it all finished."

She grabbed them both, "In fact we would like to go outside and work on it some more, right now!"

The boys took out after her and met their mother at the corner of the stairs, "Oh no you're not young man." Their mother insisted, "You're not going, running off with all of your company still here."

Joseph explained, "We'll be right back were just going up to our room for a minute."

The three raced upstairs and plopped down on Joseph's bed, "Phew! That was close!" James confessed.

Maria asked, "James? Can we see your pet rock again?"

James pulled a small rock out of his pants-pocket and placed it in the middle of the bed.

The three stared for a moment at the intricate carvings on the small hard stone. Suddenly, in the half-blink of an eye the head of the toad appeared to turn and look up at them and returned to stone.

Maria nodded, "I think it's been long enough guys. Tonight, let's go back and check out that old house on the hill."

CHAPTER 52

THURSDAY NIGHT

Sure enough, when the children got to the treehouse, the sapling is gone. At the top of the hill, behind the tree they saw a late seventeen-hundreds federal style mansion. Very much like that of Federal Hill at the My Old Kentucky Home State Park. A two-story house with its broad, newly painted, black wooden shutters, nicely trimmed hedges and a well-kept lush lawn that gave it an air of inspiring gracious hospitality.

At each end of the house, smoke drifted lazily up through the air from the two chimneys. The two enormous white columns that supported the porch were so big they seemed to hold the surrounding wilderness at bay. Box-lined walk-ways between flowering beds mediated between the house and the land.

All of it was very visually appealing like a very civilized and pleasurable way of life. It comforted the eye to an otherwise isolated range of Blue Mountains in the background.

On the ridge, far to the right, rows of fruit trees grew on the slope that dropped away sharply behind the house. More than sixty apple trees shaded the hillside all the way to the creek below. To the left, a garden laid out in precise squares. Intersected by paths and bordered with close-trimmed, wooden boxes.

The well-kept rectilinear ground plan, created a romantic sight imposing order on a very real wilderness. Even the trees were used as part of the scheme; rigidly pruned and bordered with small flowering plants. Beautifully shaped walkways surrounded the grounds, with fig trees and pecans bordering the wider paths on either side.

Stout English Yew trees poised all around the estate, a distinguishing feature of the gardens like the May Duke Cherry orchards beside them. The planning and supervision of such a garden were evident, this required both knowledge and constant care.

The working part of the mansion was not under one roof; it was the plantation street. Here was the Smokehouse, Dairy Barn, Horse stable, metal working shop, wood working shop, the Icehouse, Weaver's hut, Stonecutters Barn, and most certainly the house servants' quarters. Typically, this "street" consisted of a double file of outbuildings, including a Schoolhouse.

The main house was the center of a small village rather than a single independent dwelling. For such housekeeping, time and many hands were needed, and both were in abundant supply.

Four black women are beating the dust out of an old rug that is hanging from a heavy iron rod. This bolted rod extends from the side of the house and bent down into the ground.

Three other old black women are washing clothes in a heated kettle and hanging them on a clothes-line and an old black man with a stick is walking a horse, also five people hoeing at a garden.

Suddenly, the children see a young black girl running and playing on the hillside in front of them.

As she came rolling down the hill, she noticed them in the tree. She's wearing a dark-red and dirty white, torn plaid dress.

A lovely, little voice sounded out from below their treehouse, "What are you doing hiding up in that tree there?" It was the young girl.

It startled Maria that people could see her, talk to her -ask her to give an account of herself. While she wondered how to answer that question.

Joseph spoke up, "We're not hiding, this is our treehouse."

The young girl stared at them in the trees, "What on earth, is a, a tree house?"

From where the young girl stood, all she could see were three children climbing in a large tree.

James climbed down and stood in front of the little girl, "Hi, what's your name?"

He was wearing his favorite midnight blue sweat shirt and matching pants with black and blue Air Jordan tennis shoes.

"Hello, my name's Emma." The girl said with a slight bow, "What's your name, sir?"

James smiled, "James Michael Glover."

Emma smiled back but avoided looking into his eyes, "I'm not allowed to climb trees sir, but I don't really have anyone to play with, would y'all play with me?"

With the idea of another girl to play with, Joseph quickly climbed down and stood with James and Emma, "Maria, come down here!"

Joseph was wearing a black polyester collared shirt, old Levi blue jeans with a hole in the knee and grass-stained Converse tennis shoes.

Maria hesitated for a moment to watch James and the little girl talking.

She was wearing her forest green tee-shirt, Levi blue jeans and dark brown cotton flats.

James continued, "What's your *last* name, Emma?"

The young black girl smiled, "We don't have last names sir, don't you know only white folks got last names, but my momma she was free, her name was Sonja Jo Clarkston."

Emma spoke her mother's name with an exaggerated amount of pride, and Maria climbed down out of the treehouse.

As they walk back up the hill, Maria whispered to herself, "Emma, Emma Branham?"

"No ma'am." Emma corrected, "Master Branham is the *owner* here."

Maria asked, "You mean *your* dad owns this house?"

Emma blushed, "Don't nobody know who my father was and it most certainly never be Master Troy sir, that would be just unheard of."

Maria tried to stop the two boys, "Don't you guys?"

James interrupted, "Emma, can we ride a horse?"

Emma grinned, "Sir, those horses is for working, but I can show y'all a horse what's made for riding."

Emma took off running, "Come on now, I'll show you Big Ben, he's the Master's riding horse, he's powerful proud of Big Ben!"

Far to the left of the plantation house and all of its commotion, are a large white barn and very tall cedar posts, fencing in the largest brown horse they had ever seen.

"Wow," Exclaimed James!

Emma smiled, "That's, Big Ben."

James excitedly at Emma, "Can we pet him?"

Emma put her left hand on her hips, "Pet him, Sir, we came to feed him."

They all walk up and Emma approached the big iron gate, "He likes grass best." Emma said kneeling down.

She started grabbing handfuls of grass that are growing just outside the long reach of the big brown steed. The boys also start pulling all the tall grass they can hold in their hands. Then they watch as Emma feeds the horse.

Emma whispered, "There, Ben, you eat up now."

Maria looked at Joseph, "You know who this is, don't you?" Joseph shook his head with his eyes fixed on the large animal.

Maria stood in front of the tall boy, "Right before school-break, we had to read about this little girl that lived way back, in like, eighteen sixty-five or something; we had to read about her in *history* class remember?"

Joseph looked at Maria with amazement, while she continued to explain, "What would you say if I told you this *is* that little girl?"

Joseph just stood there shaking his head, "Is that possible?"

Maria nodded her head, "Is it possible to travel to an exponentially digressing treehouse that just appears out of nowhere?"

Joseph shut his hanging jaw. He slowly looked the familiar surroundings over. He could claim it impossible but everything fit.

James turned, "Is exponentially really a real word?"

Joseph looked at Emma, "So wait...the old house is the Branham plantation?"

James's mouth dropped open in horror, "You mean she's the little girl who got killed by." He's words suddenly cut short by Joseph's elbow in his ribs.

Emma shocked, "You mean somebody is gonna, murder me, but why?"

Maria turned Emma around, "You got," She pauses for a moment and then continued, "I mean you're *going to*!"

Joseph stopped her, "Maria - Maria, we are changing history?"

Emma's eyes opened wide, "Are you all real time-travelers just like in Mark Twain?"

Maria shook her head with confidence, "Maybe we're supposed to Joseph."

She looked at the now puzzled little girl, "Emma, you're going to be beaten to death by your father."

The startled little black girl stepped back, "My daddy, is gonna come back, lawd sakes, why would he wanna hurt me?"

CHAPTER 53

The three children were in it knee-deep and rising by the sentence. They could have walked away, back up in the treehouse, trip over a stump, and they wouldn't have to deal with this. She knew James and Joseph were thinking the same thing, or at least she hoped Joseph was. James seemed more intrigued, more willing to play it out. Without warning, he suddenly threw it all out on the table.

James stepped in front of her "Emma, Troy Branham is your dad and...and he gets drunk one day -he blames you for Sonja Clarkston's death."

The confused little child fell down in the tall grass by the fence. Emma just sits puzzled as she tries to wrap her mind around what has just been said.

Emma looked at James with surprise, "We gotta tell Mama Gertie about all this!"

She jumped up and started running down the hill, the children ran to catch up with her. They follow Emma as she ran through a huge white barn. The cool dusty air was a bit of a relief from the hot sun that had been beating down on them. The silence inside brought them all back to the reality that none of them really belonged here.

Maria stopped Emma inside the barn, "Emma we can't be seen by *anybody* around here."

Joseph nodded, "If anyone knows we're here they might take us to Captain Branham."

Maria asked, "Emma, if you go tell Gertie what we've told you, what's she going to do?"

Emma thought fast, "I could hide y'all behind the woodpile, nobody ever goes back there."

Quickly, Emma led them to the other-side of the barn. Suddenly, she is stopped by an older black man who is walking a horse.

"Emma who you talkin' to?" The man questioned.

He is wearing the usual attire for Workhands, an old hempen coarse linen short sleeve shirt and trousers and old worn-out leather shoes.

The other children are still standing just inside the barn.

"Nobody!" She looked back into the barn at the three children, "I mean I was just talking to myself." Emma is swinging the barn door back and forth.

The man sternly, "Emma you got to get your head outta them clouds, Master sir, he's been lookin' for you and you ain't been nowhere to be found!"

The old man is standing just outside the barn door. Emma is still swinging it back and forth, "I'm on my way back, so go on and walk your ole Clementine!"

He stamped his walking stick in the dusty ground, "He says he's gonna wall'op you a goodin', Emma!"

She paused for a moment. Emma understood what he was referring to when he said 'wallop'. Lola explained in class one day that John Charles Wallop, the third Earl of England who was known from an early age to have an unsound mind and violently whipped his servants often, which is the same way her master was known to handle his servants.

She remembered Miss Lola taught her that the Earl was also said to show an unusual interest in funerals, which he referred to as black-jobs. Sir Wallop attended them frequently; insisting on tolling the bells himself and violently flogged any other ringers with the bell-rope.

So, when Mister Toby said that, she understood the violent beating she might receive from her Master Troy; however, Emma didn't have time to think of herself, the safety of her new friends was the only thing on her mind.

Emma slammed the barn door, "Oh go on Toby, Gertie told me not to take any lip offin' the likes a you! And if Miss Lola saw you totin' that stick like a cane, she'd beat you with it!"

The old man shook his head and turned away. As he walked down past the barn with the horse, he whispered under his breath, "Youngins today, got no respect for their elders!"

Emma opened the barn door all the way, "Come on I'll take you guys where no one will ever find you."

The four take off running down the hillside. Half out of breath Emma turns to James, "You all hide here behind this ole wood pile, don't nobody ever come back here!"

"But, Emma!" Maria tried to stop her.

Emma yelled, "Y'all stay hidden, you can't be seen in those clothes, being from the future an all!"

Emma ran past all the tall piles of wood with tears in her eyes, "My Mamma, and Master sir?"

Emma ran across the small wooden bridge over a deep running stream, when she saw her Master Troy and young Mister William stomping toward her. Emma remembered she was supposed to be helping Miss Nilda clean the upstairs, but she had been playing with the Glover children all day.

Troy is wearing an unbuttoned black dress-coat with the full collar rolling low, white vest, black doeskin pantaloons and stout soled black shoes.

Suddenly with a voice that trembled Emma to her bones, "Emma!" Her master bellowed out, "I have been looking all over for you for almost an hour!"

William voiced, "I told you sir; she would be playing on the woodpile!"

He was wearing his usual brown shawl-collared, single-breasted wool vest under his black double-breasted Brooks Brothers wool coat, black wool high-knee trousers, white wool stockings and polished black leather shoes.

The young man might appear to be somewhat of a tattle-tail but from his point of view, he saw Emma as a representative of their people and of their gods and he felt she should be perfect. In fact, he held everyone in such high regard; He expected everyone to be perfect.

"You wait right here William!" The staggering master ordered as he swung the whip in his hand.

"My Father?" Emma whispered to herself shaking her head, fearfully clutching something in the pocket of her apron.

CHAPTER 54

She silently pleaded with the great gods to let the master have mercy on her; silently begging the charm to bring its magic forth quickly and save her. Somehow, she knew this was to be a beating that would make all others pale in comparison.

-She felt it.

Master Branham grabbed Emma by the arm and halfway across the bridge, the pocket on her tattered apron caught upon a rough railing. Emma almost fell with the jerk it caused when the pocket -pulled off.

Trying to save herself, she forgot she was clutching her magic toad. In horror, she heard it 'plunk' -into the murky water below!

He dragged her out behind the stockpile of logs. As Emma quickly looked around, she didn't see the children anywhere and that was where Troy lost all control. The stress of the day had built up too much for him to handle any longer. The whip thrashed against her poor little body. Though she screamed and begged him to stop, he acted as one deaf.

Finally, Maria ran out from behind the heap of lumber and threw herself over the crying little girl. Guarding Emma with her own body.

She screamed up at him from the top of her lungs, "Killing Emma won't bring her mother back!" Tears ran down Maria's face.

Troy stood there with his fist still in the air. After a moment he fell to his knees and burst out with tears in his eyes. The drunken Master snatched Emma up in his arms and held her, "I can't believe I almost killed my only child!"

Joseph and James came out from behind their hiding places. Maria stood up and wrapped her arms around Joseph's neck. The sky started to sprinkle with the tears of Ogun.

James looked up at them and wrapped his arms around them both, "We changed history!" James blurted out.

Maria burst out a giggle through her tears and hugged James's around the neck.

Suddenly, Maria felt something brush up around her ankle. When she looked down, there was a white cat, "Sophie?" She said through her tears of joy. Maria instantly recognized her neighbor's cat and picked the animal up into her arms.

"Sophie? That's *your* cat?" Emma's eyes lit up, "I've learned so much from her." Emma said as she ran her fingers over the cats matted fur.

-Maria motioned for her to take the cat.

"Oh, no!" Emma confessed, "Cats don't live very long around here! Some of the superstitious Workhands have been trying to kill poor Sophie for near a month now."

The children look at each other and after a moment Maria smiled and looked at her wristwatch, "Oh no!"

James cried out, "What, what happened now?"

"We've been here for almost four hours!" Maria explained.

James looked at Joseph, "So how long has it been -in our time?"

"Maybe like a week!" Maria cried out, "Or longer who knows, maybe even a year!"

Joseph looked at her, "Exponentially it could even be a hundred years!"

James with a depressing look, lowers his head, "So if we go back now, Mom is already old or dead?"

Joseph nodded his head, "Everything we know of is, is gone?"

Emma's face clouded with disappointment as she walked up to James, "I wish I had my magic toad I could've helped you all." Emma bowed her head, "but I lost it forever in the stream."

James reached into his pocket, "You mean like this one?" He showed her a rock in the shape of a frog. The warm sprinkling rain increased.

Emma amazed, "My charm, you found it!" as he hands Emma the Granite Toad.

Maria held Sophie tight in her arms, while Emma stroked the rock with her finger, *"Wind a change, sand a time, send them back, these friends of mine."*

Troy turned to see William walking up from behind. Suddenly, the three children glow and disappear into a dim radiant flash of green light. When Troy turned around, the children were gone, "Emma, one day you're going to have to tell me, just exactly what happened here?"

In a heavy downpour Emma smiled and wrapped her skinny little arms tightly around her father's neck and whispered to herself, "Thank you Ogun." The sun shining overhead.

Today was the greatest day of her life. She finally got to hug the neck of her father. That meant more to her than anything else that was going on, because sometimes, the only one who can fix a broken-heart is the one who broke it.

CHAPTER 55

The three children find themselves back in the lot, but it's so dark they can't even see their hands in front of their face.

Joseph spoke up, "What time do you think it is?" Stumbling over something at his feet.

James realized he is in a room. "That clock says 11:00 P.M."

"What are y'all doing in my bedroom?" A voice said in the dark.

"Emma?" James whispered.

Suddenly, they heard a gasp and a light came on. They are standing in a girl's bedroom, with pink and blue paint on the walls. A big stuffed bear is sitting in a rocking-chair by an open closet.

A young black girl is standing in the middle of her bed wearing a two-piece Buffalo Check coat-style fleece pajamas. Her hand still on the light switch, "Are y'all the Glover kids, you've been on the news for days?"

Bright-green wooden letters are over her bed that reads. "D A R I E N" in all capital letters.

"Darien?" Maria spoke up, "We can't explain how we got here!" She confessed, petting the cat in her arms.

Darien put her hand on her hip, "Try me!"

They all three sat down and start explaining how it all happened. A magical story of how they came to be in Darien's bedroom.

Joseph looked at Maria, "Even though I was there, I have to admit this still sounds impossible to believe."

As crazy as the story was, Darien spoke up, "I believe it!"

"You do?" James asked.

"Yep!" Darien nodded, "My daddy's been telling me this tale ever since I was little. How do you all know *that* story?"

James blurted, "We were there!"

Darien sat down, "Wait! Are you telling me, you three are the same kids my great, great-grandfather saw?"

Maria and Joseph look at each other for a moment as the young girl turned and got a flashlight out of her nightstand drawer.

James commented, "Hey Joseph, she keeps a flashlight in her nightstand just like you."

"Darn it!" Darien complained, "My batteries are dead!"

The two boys look at each other in disbelief, "The batteries!" Joseph pulled a package of fresh batteries from his pocket and hands them to Darien.

James whispered, "But how, how could he know we were going to need them, how did he know?"

They sneak out of the girls' house and out into the yard. A comfortable humming can be heard from the transformer overhead. Birds are chirping in the distance.

Darien asked with a humble sincerity, "Will you guys come over and play with me? There hasn't been anybody here to play with since I moved in?"

Maria smiled at her, "Oh course, Darien, we'll always come over, but I have a feeling we might be grounded, for a very, very long time."

"Oh no," James said, "We've been gone for, for days? Wait, how long have we been gone?"

Darien shook her head, "Two days!"

Maria spoke up, "Today is only Sunday, night?"

She let Sophie hop down onto the frosty morning dirt and the animal quickly ran toward the boy's backyard.

"Wow!" Joseph said, "They built your house, really fast!"

"Not really." Darien explained, "It's a pre-fab! A modular home?"

"But, all the lumber?" Maria questioned.

Darien nodded, "That's for the garage, it's still not finished."

Maria looked over at Joseph, "That might be our fault, we stole some of your lumber to fix our treehouse."

Darien's eyes lit up, "You guys have a treehouse? That's awesome!"

"No." James said with a discouraged tone, "I think it's gone."

They all four turned to look back at the thin row of trees that separated Darien's yard from the subdivision on the next street. Somehow those houses didn't seem so far away anymore and the idea of playing in the next neighborhood felt -almost inviting.

In the shadows of the early morning the white cat could barely be seen as she gracefully walking down the top of the fence that separates the boys and Dr. Bonzon's backyard. Sophie jumped down into the yard and silently leaped up in the doctors Livingroom window.

"Troy, Troy." She voiced.

The Livingroom window slowly raised up and she quickly leaped inside.

Inside the house the man's voice spoke up, "Kumusta gwapa. Welcome home Sophie, darling. What have you been into tonight night?"

The old man slowly closed his window.

CHAPTER 56

MONDAY MORNING

April 8th, 1985

The ride on the bus this morning was filled with fuzzy memories of their last night's adventure. All they could do was, tell their parents that they got lost. The truth, was so much more than they could deal with and their lie was the only thing that helped them cope with their memories.

The three walked into school just as they have done for the past five months but today, they felt like it was the very first time. Everything was the same but somehow everyone seemed so different.

Somehow, they could tell how someone felt, just by the expressions on their face. This was something they never noticed before. Instead of judging people by, how they looked and what they wore, suddenly they could read what people were thinking because everyone's thoughts were all over their face.

Before school started, all of the students were gathering in the front lobby, where they stood around and talked until First Period. Today, unlike every day the Gentleman's Restroom was blocked by a table with a note that read, "Out of Order." According to the passing murmurs, the bathroom was off-limits because a girl threw-up in there but why a girl was in the Boy's Restroom was still a mystery.

Joseph really had to pee badly and took one look at the note and blasted, "Out of order? I've got to piss!"

With a pointed finger at the sign "You're, out of order!" and he slid over the table and went into the restroom.

For the past five months he has gone unnoticed by just about everybody in the entire school. So, he was under the impression that no one will notice him now. Believing that no one saw him, he went about his business of relieving himself and washing his hands. However, upon leaving the restroom he was greeted by two younger boys and rounds of applause by several children that were standing in the lobby.

One boy stood there wearing a black T-shirt, Levi blue-jeans, Nike tennis-shoes and one earring in his left ear. His long dark brown hair hung past his shoulders.

"Holy shit dude!" The boy expressed, "Everybody thought about doing that and a lot of people said they might, but you man, you just walked right in there!"

The other boy was wearing a collared pastel blue button-up Polo shirt, tan khaki pants and brown leather shoes.

"Yea man!" The other boy voiced, "You got balls of steel!"

Joseph glanced out at the lobby and noticed the school's custodian was eyeing him with a frown but only stood there – saying nothing.

He walked to where he would ordinarily be standing at this time of day. Usually, he would be leaning up against the wall near the two big closed wooden doors that lead to the class rooms, waiting for the doors to open so he could go to homeroom class.

This is where he stood every single morning for the last five months, but today he felt different. He couldn't bring himself to just stand there, leaning up against that damn wall.

When he turned around there were those two boys again, "Hey man, what's your name?" Joseph wasn't really used to this kind of attention but then again, he wasn't really himself today.

"I can't tell you that." Joseph said calmly, "I would have to kill you! And then find a place to hide the bodies! -I'm not in the mood."

The two boys laughed, "I love this guy, man! He's so cool!"

Joseph walked past them muttering, "I desperately wish there was a place to sit down around here."

The other boy explained, "There is a place to sit down, at the center of the lobby."

"Now they tell me!" Joseph exclaimed.

There was a large stone seat that went all the way around a huge stone column, right where they said it would be. There he saw James and Maria, sitting very comfortably and talking amongst themselves.

As he sat down, he noticed there was a school News Paper, picked it up and started reading, "Yea guys does anything seems unusual about today?"

"I feel so relaxed." James said with a smile.

Maria whispered, "Are we just so *jaded* by what happened, that nothing affects us now?"

Joseph read aloud, "After lunch, in the lobby today, we are selling soft-drinks for a quarter to help raise money for the cheerleaders!"

Maria spoke up, "I thought I wanted to be a cheerleader but today *school* seems so far ways."

James spoke up, "Where's Darien, she wasn't on the bus?"

Joseph once again read aloud from the newspaper, "If anyone would like to join cheerleaders, Dawn Jewel will be in the gym, fifth period, accepting tryouts."

Maria voiced, "I feel such a heavy weight lifted off me that I didn't even realize was there."

Out of the corner of James eyes he realized a group of children about his age. They were watching his every move and whispered to each other. He could have easily just sat there and ignored them, like he had done, for so long but right this very minute he wasn't himself anymore and had no idea who he was.

When he turned and got up, one boy about his height with brown hair and green eyes, stood there while a girl stood holding her breath.

The girl was wearing silver earrings under her short blonde curly hair, Pastel pink and white all polyester matching blouse and knee-high skirt, long white stockings and tulip double-strapped leather shoes.

After a pause James spoke up, "What 'cha doin'?"

With a blast, the boy explained, "We are trying to see who can hold their breath the longest! So far, she can hold her breath for almost thirty minutes!"

The boy was wearing a collared mustard-yellow all cotton shirt, dark-brown corduroy pants and Dollar Store brand tennis shoes.

James knew from common knowledge that most athletic swimmers can only hold their breath for no more than a little over eleven minutes, and this little porker was no athlete. Immediately he understood the girl was not holding her breath, just merely standing there, with cheeks puffed out and gently breathing through her nose.

"She's a fraud!" He bellowed out.

He gently pinched her nose-holes together and quickly the girl started gasping for breath. Laughter filled the lobby as James noticed the other children gathering around him. They couldn't wait to see what he was going to do next.

-Finally, the first-period bell rang.

CHAPTER 57

"Kiss of the Cupid Stone."

All of the student are now leaving the lobby and heading down the hallways, leading to the many classrooms. Metal lockers lined the walls and after stopping off at one to get things for class, Joseph was on his way with book in hand.

A very beautiful blonde girl was standing in the hall. She was wearing an all-cotton T-shirt, Levi blue-jeans and Nike tennis-shoes.

She stood there sobbing while four boys were looking around on the floor. With both hands, she quickly grabbed Joseph by the shirt collar.

"If anybody can help me, it has to be you!" She spoke.

Joseph shocked, "What did you lose?"

She wrapped her arms around him tightly, "I can't find my stone!"

"Dude, she lost something off her necklace!" One boy instructed. The boy was wearing a black all cotton T-shirt, Wrangler blue-jeans and Dollar Store tennis shoes.

"No! ...Man, she lost a charm off her bracelet!" Another boy argued. He was wearing a white collared all cotton polo shirt, Jordache blue-jeans and Nike tennis-shoes.

Joseph glanced back to her, "Where were you when you lost it?"

The short girl looked up into his eyes, "You are the first guy, to ask me that. Everybody else just assumed I lost it right here."

This reminded him of a joke where a guy was looking for a quarter outside because it was too dark inside the movie theater.

Joseph grabbed her by both arms with a squint toward the boys, "Is this just a joke?"

A brunette-haired girl walked by, "That's nothing, I lost my little red marble!" She was wearing a black T-shirt with the image of AC/DC on the breast, Levi blue-jeans and Dollar Store tennis shoes.

The blonde-haired girl pleaded, "Would you please help me find it?"

"What does it look like?" Joseph asked.

"You know!" She insisted, "It's a, a Cupid Stone!" She gazed into his eyes, "It's a perfect Cupid Stone! It was the only one I've ever had. -The only one I ever cared about."

She glanced at the other four boys, who were now standing there staring at them. She grabbed Joseph by the collar and tugged for him to follow her around the corner.

"This is the very spot where I ...I lost it! ...I just totally lost it!" She exclaimed.

Joseph was getting the impression, she was trying to tell him that she lost control of herself, over something that happened -in this very spot.

He shook his head, "Okay, okay! First of all, I would like to personally apologize, for the way he treated you."

She was completely shocked by that statement. It left her utterly speechless for a moment. She still had a hold of his shirt when she collapsed down to her knees. Joseph knelt down in front of her. Suddenly, she broke down into tears and started bawling her eyes out. Everyone in the hall got very quiet.

"If you don't mind me being nosy." Joseph spoke softly, "Could you please tell me what his name is?"

She looked at him with tears in her eyes, she finally confessed, "I don't know what his name is."

"Well." Joseph said, "Can you show me what your perfect cupid stone looks like?"

She took her finger and placed it between his upper lip, "This spot." She explained, "Is called your Cupid Stone."

She took a deep breath through her nose as she deeply pressed her warm, wet lips against his. A hot sensation swept up the back of his neck and goose-bumps ran down both of his arms.

A long resounding, "Damn!" A boy voiced over the crowd.

Just then the bell rang for class to start and the girl jumped up, and ran down the hall. Joseph just sat there on the floor for a moment, with a hot face and rosy cheeks.

He happened to look down and noticed a small red marble by his shoe. He smiled for a moment at the small round piece of glass, like it was a souvenir of his first kiss and put it in his pocket.

He realized he was alone in the hall when he finally pulled himself together and staggered to his class. Everyone was already at their desk and staring at him with whispers. He floated in and sat down with his head still in the clouds.

CHAPTER 58

Today is the first day of school, after a long spring break. The children have a new found sense of pride in their History Class because, now they not only feel like they know a bit more about history, they also hope they may have changed it along the way. A sense of a more advanced mental and emotional maturity grew from their adventure and the children feel so much more connected to the day.

The teacher spoke over the noise, "Good morning, class! I would like to introduce you to Miss Darien Watson! Her parents just moved here from Kentucky and she is going to be our new student."

-Meanwhile, in the back of the class.

A girl sitting in front of Maria held most of the conversation around her, "I like putting grapes and bananas in my Fruit Loop cereal."

The girl was wearing a pastel-blue all polyester blouse, Guess blue-jeans and Nike tennis-shoes.

Another girl spoke up, "I like to put several different kinds of cereals in my Fruit Loops."

The first girl turned around and noticed Maria was listening, "Do you like Fruit Loops?" The girl asked.

She glanced around and noticed everyone stopped talking to listen to what Maria was going to say.

Maria nodded her head, "I put diamonds, in my Fruit Loops -makes my shit twinkle."

The laughter of everyone around her quickly ended when the teacher spoke up, "Now Darien, since you are new here, I don't expect you to know the answers to these questions!"

After a moment she continued, "All, right, class, who can tell me who Emma's father was?"

A young girl in the front row raised her hand, "Charles Branham the second."

"That's right!" The teacher said.

Maria shook her head, "Actually Miss Whitfield, it was Troy Eugene Branham the second, *Charles* Branham was her grandfather."

Maria's long silky brown hair was tied up in a ponytail with a blue and white scrunchy that matched her pastel-blue and white patterned, high-neck cotton sweater and pastel-blue slacks. Her brand new, all white Nike tennis shoes, neatly laced with pastel-blue shoe strings.

The teacher looked at her papers, "I'll have to check my book, but I think you might be right Maria. Now class, number twelve, who was Sonja Jo Clarkston?"

Joseph raised his hand, "Emma's mother." He looked very handsome sitting there in his dark-blue button up short-sleeve collared shirt, tan corduroy slacks and Adidas tennis shoes.

The teacher impressed, "Very good, Joseph, I can see you three studied over spring break. Okay, class number thirteen, *when* did Emma Watson die?"

They all three looked at each other with the sorrowful idea that time might not have been changed. Darien in the front row looked at Maria and Joseph and then raised her hand.

"Yes, Darien?" The teacher acknowledged.

The young black girl was wearing a delicately designed pastel peach over-sized cotton blouse, Pastel purple corduroy slacks and brown leather shoes.

Darien stood up in class and cleared her throat, "Emma Branham Watson lived to be eighty-one years old and helped petition congress about the Thirteenth Amendment on April eighth eighteen eighty-eight, to help abolish slavery and the encouragement of equality."

"Well, thank you, Miss. Watson, but all I needed to here was the year; now class number fourteen!"

"Oh!" Darien blushed, "nineteen twenty-seven." And sat back down.

Joseph and Maria look at each other with a pleasing grin.

Joseph mouthed silently, "nineteen, twenty-seven."

CHAPTER 59

MONDAY AFTERNOON

As the four children were walking home, they felt completely awake. They were utterly aware of everything around them. Maria looked on the ground, the rocks she was walking on were the same old rocks she has always walked on since she moved here but right this very moment, they seemed super-real. The sun shined on them like a spotlight. She looked up into the trees -Everything looked so green.

The sound of the birds chirping and the wind blowing. It seemed so quiet compared to the day they've all had. The day was cloudy but the sun seemed to peer directly over them. As they walked, the opening in the clouds followed and a small pin-hole shined down. The sunbeam seemed to only shine on them.

They noticed Dr. Bonzon, sitting in a chair on his front porch and Sophie sitting patiently in his lap while he brushed the tangles out of her fur.

The children waved as they walked by and Sophie jumped down and started eating out of her food bowl.

Maria yelled from the white picket fence, "Kumusta Tito, I see she has her appetite back!"

The happy doctor slowly shook his head and sat rocking with a smile on his face.

Darien yelled, "Race you to my house!" and the children take off running.

All four of them are now in Darien's backyard; Joseph is surprised to find their favorite climbing rock was still here, "They didn't get rid of it?"

Darien smiled as she squats down beside him, "That's what I wanted to talk to you about. This thing was so big my dad just decided to leave it here."

Maria asked, "Hey guys, did you notice everyone was so different today?"

Darien nodded, "After all this time it's never occurred to you, you've been on the news since last Friday. -you're all famous!"

Maria noticed something she has never seen before, engraved in the stone's side were old markings of several large letters, "Emma Loves James?......1871!" The young girl blurted out with ecstatic amazement.

Even though Emma had never explained to her father anything that happened that day, she still asked someone to place a huge granite slab in the very spot where those three children stood. Her good friend, Mister Jonathan was a very skilled Stonecutter and the part of the stone that read "1871" seemed to be cleverly away from the rest of the slab. As James pushed on it, the whole thing gracefully slid out like a stone drawer. In it they saw various items, much like a time capsule.

Joseph reached in, "My flashlight?"

Maria smiled at him and then looked back into the tiny compartment, "James, do you see what I see?"

His little eyes gazed over into the drawer at the many things Emma left there; an arrowhead, a book by Mark Twain, some old coins.

Then he suddenly saw it, "My frog!" He yelled out as he reached in, "My pet frog!"

CHAPTER 60

To an adult it looked like nothing more than a rock, but through the eyes of a young child it was a magical Granite Toad. Though my hands have never held that small black stone that blessed their youth or possessed the magical ability that would take me far into the future. However, I have, always kept the thoughts of that day with me at all times.

Some of those memories, of who I was, when I was young, have never left me. One cannot always choose their environment, but for the most part, my life is what I make it.

Those years of living on the ole Branham plantation were never about being a servant. It was about having a purpose. My life as a young man, growing up there was always filled with the love of family. If not by our own blood, then by the blood of Jesus Christ, we were all family. We prospered together in those trying times. Life was hard and simple but that was the way many people grew-up and it seems to me now, life was even more grand that way. Aside from the hustle and bustle of the crazy world that was going on beyond our haven in the Blue Ridge mountains of West Virginia.

Throughout my entire life, all of my memories have always been on Emma and those three children who may have saved her life that day.

When Emma and her husband had their first child, she named him William Troy Watson. This young man passed down the legend I lay before you now.

These are the accounts that I bear witness to and testify that they are as accurate as I can remember. Because we were there to witness them, and all the magical moments of Emma's childhood.

Sincerely yours, Mr. William G. Watson III

CHAPTER 61

The ambiance of creek water gently tinkled in the distance, and the wind softly blew through the leaves on the big old Oak tree. The air smelled fresh like a morning in spring, but still something seemed so unreal about this place.

In the distance, Joseph, Maria and Darien are up in the treehouse, taking turns jumping and floating from one branch to another while James is standing on the ground, talking to a six-year-old girl. Her curly blonde hair falling down around the shoulders of her long-sleeve pastel white petticoat dress with pink ruffles that went all the way down to her ankles.

"Hello, what is your name?" James asked.

The girl smiled, "Angela. What's yours?"

James stood there in his long black cape and matching pajamas, "I'm Bat Man."

CHAPTER 62

Emma Branham Watson was born, May seventeenth, eighteen sixty-two near West Virginia. Her father was a very wealthy Captain and landowner. He eventually found love in his life, in the eyes of someone who grew closest to him. Troy and Nilda were married in the spring of April 26th 1874.

When Troy passed away in the winter of nineteen o one, his only child inherited the responsibility of "Freedom for All". A slogan that cannot be found in history books today.

Nilda Caintic Branham finally returned to Tacloban Leyte Philippines where she was reunited with her family and friends.

Emma eventually married a well-educated black man named Doctor Joseph Watson. Joseph was one of the few free-men in his time, which had the fortune of being taught to read and write by his owners and graduated at the University of Virginia in 1882.

In Emma's lifetime, she had been persecuted, and imprisoned many times. Mrs. Watson was known for quoting Leonardo da Vinci when he once said, "Nothing strengthens authority so much as silence."

She died in her spring-home from health complications in the summer of nineteen twenty-seven, and left behind a legacy of her memories through her children that will hopefully live on in our hearts for years to come.